Dear Readers,

This time of year, there are plenty of reasons to celebrate—so why not add four spectacular new romances from Bouquet to your list?

Sometimes love turns up even when you're not looking for it. In beloved author Colleen Faulkner's **Taming Ben,** a determined bachelor tries to remember why he objects to relationships when he hires a painter with a heart as big as her smile. Of course, no man can be a **Solitary Man** forever—as the rugged Boston cop in Karen Drogin's emotional offering discovers when his partner's sister shows him why two is better than one.

Next, rising star Suzanne Barrett presents **Hearts At Risk.** When a man who's decided to retreat from the corporate world to his rural family estate finds that a charming woman has a long-term lease on the caretaker's cottage, the first seeds of romance are planted. And last, in **The Littlest Matchmaker** by Laura Phillips, a charming four-year-old is determined to find herself a new mommy, and the manager of the hotel where she and her tycoon father have set up camp is the perfect choice—if only she can convince them to choose love before business. . . .

Enjoy!

Kate Duffy
Editorial Director

HEARTS AT RISK

SUZANNE BARRETT

Zebra Books
Kensington Publishing Corp.
http://www.zebrabooks.com

ZEBRA BOOKS are published by

Kensington Publishing Corp.
850 Third Avenue
New York, NY 10022

All Kensington Titles, Imprints, and Distributed Lines are available at special quantity discounts for bulk purchases for sales
promotions, premiums, fund-raising, and educational or institu-
tional use. Special book excerpts or customized printings can also
be created to fit specific needs. For details, write or phone the
office of the Kensington special sales manager: Kensington Publishing Corp., 850 Third Avenue, New York, NY 10022, attn:
Special Sales Department, Phone: 1-800-221-2647.

Zebra and the Z logo Reg. U.S. Pat. & TM Off.

First Printing: December, 2000
10 9 8 7 6 5 4 3 2 1

Printed in the United States of America

for Ann La Farge

Acknowledgments

Caro and Bruce. Keep working the magic.

ONE

April Fairchild stared in disbelief at the letter she'd ripped open with her garden shears. "Who does this McKittrick fellow think he is?" She crumpled the paper and shoved it into the pocket of her smock. "The trouble with corporate executives," she muttered to the black-and-white cat batting at her shoelace, "is they can't see beyond their high-rise office windows."

She seized her pruners and snipped a damaged cane off the Docteur du Jamain. In another week, the rose would be covered in fragrant, dark-red blooms, but it wouldn't matter one bit if the new owner ordered her off the property. Her throat tightened. It wasn't fair.

She sidestepped a fat mackerel tabby poised to pounce on something—probably her ragged sneaker—and clipped a wayward shoot from the pale ivory Sombreuil that skimmed the stone wall bordering the caretaker's cottage.

If Mr. Thomas J. McKittrick wants me off the estate, it'll take more than a note from his pushy attorney. She brushed back a strand of blond hair that had come loose from the flat tortoiseshell barrette at her nape. No way

would she give up six years of her life without a fight.
He'd have to use force.

She fished in her pocket for the letter and reread the
opening paragraph. "We expect you to vacate the property known as Creggan no later than Monday the elev-
enth. . . ."

It made no sense. She'd just received a note from
McKittrick's office last week thanking her for her excellent payment record. The eviction notice had to be a mistake.

But there it was, plain as the eye on a potato.

She squinted at the signature. There was only one thing
to do. She'd call James Rector, Esq. this very minute.
Disengaging her shoelace from the cat, she marched toward the cottage.

In her compact, green-and-white kitchen, she dialed
the number, then juggled the handset while she plugged
in the electric kettle for tea.

"Blum, Blum, and Rector," a woman's voice intoned.

"James Rector, please." Why did all legal receptionists
sound as if they were underwater?

"He's gone for the day," the woman answered in a
nasal twang. "If you'd like to leave a message. . . ."

April groaned and waited for the voice mail beep.

She cleared her throat. "This is April Fairchild. I received your letter. However, I have a lease agreement
with Mr. Jerome McKittrick, which assures me of continued access. . . ."

She reiterated the rest of the terms and hung up. Stating her case to an answering machine did nothing to ease
the dull ache spreading from her shoulders down her
spine.

The kettle screamed. She splashed water over an Earl Grey tea bag, settled onto a green painted ladderback chair at the round kitchen table and stared at the row of potted herbs on the sunny windowsill. Sage and thyme, root cuttings of lemon verbena, lavender, and purple-blooming hyssop. All waited for planting in the newly dug herb bed. They'd perfume the air around the cottage, and when harvested, they'd be used in sachets, decoctions, and medicinal infusions.

If she could convince McKittrick's slick lawyer that she needed to stay.

Dread welled up from the pit of her stomach. She couldn't give it up. She'd come to Creggan the month after Teddy died, and the cottage had been her safe haven all this time. She'd transformed it from a drab, drafty cabin into a warm, snug home for herself and the nine stray cats she had adopted over the years.

She glanced at the photo tucked into a shelf in the open area that was her living room. Teddy Fairchild. Wealthy, handsome, reckless.

And . . . dead.

She let out the breath she'd been holding. The cottage here at Creggan had been her lifeline. She'd healed, built a new life—a life she liked. Needed, even. She couldn't give it up; it had cost her too much.

A sleek, black form brushed against her leg. Shadow, the latest of her rescues, a rail-thin, newly altered tom, demanded attention. She bent to stroke the shiny fur. She'd found him foraging in a Dumpster behind the Shady Acres convalescent home. With luck she'd find a home for him this week. For Shadow and the six other strays she'd taken in over the winter. Between tending the gardens, her dried-herb-and-flower business, and finding homes for assorted cats, her life at Creggan was full. Safe.

She glared at the crumpled letter she'd tossed onto the table.

Until today.

The bell in St. John's church tower rang out over the valley below. Six o'clock. Dinnertime for cats and for April. She stepped outside, retrieved her pruners, and tossed the rose clippings into the compost bin she'd built last summer. The sun glinted red-gold shafts of light through a stand of newly leafed-out liquidambars. April tipped her head up and squinted, letting the rays warm her face. Creggan was the most beautiful spot on earth. She had to stay. *Had to.* The cottage and her gardens not only made her herb business possible, they nourished her soul.

Old Jerome McKittrick had loved the place, too. He'd used it as a retreat from his San Francisco brokerage firm until he moved into a retirement home, at which time he'd given her a ten-year lease on the cottage. Generous use of half-timbered trim and rounded shingles gave the sprawling eighty-year-old main house a fairy tale appearance, as if Snow White herself might step through the arched doorway.

The shake-sided caretaker's cottage the old man had left her was her home and workshop. Her kingdom. The only place she'd ever felt totally at peace.

At the cottage door she called the cats, then filled three bowls with kibble. If Junior McKittrick thought he could evict her, he was nuts. She wasn't leaving, ever!

* * *

April shoved her vintage Volvo into gear and headed down the highway. At Lupine Valley's first weekly farmers' market of the season, she'd sold all but two of the eucalyptus wreaths she'd made and three dozen lavender sachets. She should be thrilled. Instead, she couldn't shake the knot of worry in the pit of her stomach. Maybe she should telephone Big Shot McKittrick himself and explain.

She swerved to avoid a pothole. Useless idea. Men like McKittrick don't care about other people's lives. They are too busy worrying about their stock market assets.

The sky darkened. Channel Four news had predicted rain, but the black clouds above looked like a real gully washer. She tightened her lips. Just what she needed. The driveway would flood again, and she'd have to call Dave to bring out his grader.

She shoved the accelerator to the floor, and the car leaped forward. She had to get home and cover the seedlings before the storm broke.

Huge raindrops began to pelt her windshield. Flipping on the wipers, she peered at the twisting road ahead and leaned the car into a curve. She pulled into her driveway and came to instant attention. Another car sat in her drive, a sleek silver Mercedes. The driver's side was empty. She slammed on the brakes.

Her skin prickled.

Thunder rumbled as she opened the door and set one foot on the ground. No one she knew owned a Mercedes. Cautiously, she climbed out of the car, shut the door, and dashed toward her front door.

A tall man appeared from behind the Rosa Mundi

hedge between her cottage and the main house. He strode across the spongy meadow, oblivious to the spray of mud gushing up with each step. Water darkened the shoulders of his suede jacket, and a shock of dark hair hung over his brow. He picked his way through the tall grass, a scowl clouding his features.

April noted his mud-spattered shoes—expensive Italian loafers. Odd for a prowler. Who was he? "What are you doing here?" she called.

The man's features hardened. "You're supposed to be gone."

Her heart thumped. "I beg your pardon?"

The man stopped three feet from her and stared into her face. "Mrs. Fairchild?"

His face, which looked as if it had been chiseled from granite, was extraordinarily handsome except for the scowl. His eyes were an odd shade, neither green nor brown, and they bored into her as if he wanted to pin her to the wall. "I am April Fairchild."

His eyebrows drew together in a frown. "You got my attorney's letter?"

His attorney's letter? Oh, Lord, was this Thomas J. McKittrick? Dumbstruck, she peered at him. A bold forehead and firm chin with the hint of a cleft. He was taller than she'd pictured him, at least six feet two. Lean, rangy build with broad shoulders, and hair that looked like it had a mind of its own. Except right now it was plastered to his head.

"I received a letter yesterday. I called Mr."—she searched her mind for the attorney's name—"Mr. Rector's office and left a message."

McKittrick studied her. "How long will it take you to vacate the cottage?"

April sucked in a breath. He couldn't be serious. She eyed the sodden front and shoulders of his jacket, the rivulet of rain running off his straight nose. She'd have a better chance of convincing him out of the rain.

"You might as well come inside. We can talk where it's dry." She led the way along the path to the front door and unlatched it.

McKittrick hesitated at the threshold, his mouth set in a grim line. She took another deep breath. "You're getting wet."

He glanced at his jacket and hesitated a moment longer. Then with a shrug he ducked under the low beam. He stood just inside in a stiff-legged stance but let his eyes wander around the room, taking in the leather chair, her plump denim sofa, and the bookshelves that ran down one side of the room. He seemed to be taking inventory.

April rubbed her arms, then knelt beside the wood-stove and added two sticks of kindling and a madrone log to the banked embers. In seconds, the kindling flared. When flames lapped the log, she turned to him.

"Look, I—" he began. Suddenly, he sneezed.

"Give me your jacket, and I'll get you a towel."

He frowned but shrugged out of the wet garment.

His jacket smelled like damp leather and something woodsy and male. Her nostrils tingled. She hung the wet suede over the back of a kitchen chair, then reached in a cupboard for a blue bath towel and handed it to him. He sneezed again and rubbed his sodden hair.

She plugged in the electric kettle and watched him. A muscular torso tapered to a narrow waist. Nice backside, too, if one were interested. She wasn't. The coffee type, she decided. She measured four scoops of French roast into the filter.

"Cream?" she asked. On second thought, he didn't seem like the cream type.

He flashed her a quick glance that turned into a look of resignation. He might as well accept her hospitality. It was raining jackhammers outside.

"Sure."

She brewed the coffee and poured out two mugs and handed one to him, motioning to the sofa.

He shook his head and stared down at the steaming liquid. "I'll stand." He raised the mug to his lips.

Uneasy, April perched on one arm of the sofa and studied him. He had long tapered fingers; she imagined them signing executive documents. He looked crisp and efficient. Starched. She gave him a wary smile and sipped her coffee.

After a long pause, he set his mug on the table. "I believe we were talking about your occupancy of the cottage."

She raised her eyes to his. *Here it comes,* she thought. "I had an agreement with your—with Jerome McKittrick."

"My grandfather. He died two years ago." He ran a hand across his forehead. "I own the estate now."

"Yes, but—"

He cut her off with a wintry stare. "I will be occupying the house from now on, Mrs. Fairchild. I've no need for a caretaker. In fact, I'd prefer to be alone."

"That's easy for you to say, but my lease—"

"Doesn't apply any longer. As I said, my grandfather's dead."

April gritted her teeth. "I understand that, Mr. McKittrick." She opened her mouth to explain about the lease, then changed her mind. No sense antagonizing the man. She struggled to keep her voice calm. "I can't just leave. This place, it's my livelihood. The roses are prizewinners, and I've hybridized three new strains. And my wreaths. . . ."

"Wreaths?" One brow quirked upward.

"I sell them at the farmer's market on Tuesdays, along with my sachets and potpourri. My herbs and flowers are my only source of income." She reached a hand toward him. "I mean this isn't just a home, Mr. McKittrick, it's my whole life!"

He gave her an odd look. "It's my land. My property."

"Yes, of course, but—"

"My estate. And my caretaker's cottage." Jaw squared, he crossed his arms in front of him. "I want you out of here."

"Well, I won't go!" She gulped at her blurted words, but she couldn't back down now. "I have a legal right to be here."

"Only until Monday," he snapped. "Read my attorney's letter."

"Of all the unreasonable, pigheaded—" She clamped her lips together. "I apologize for getting personal, but I do not apologize for stating my case." She drew in a shaky breath. "I need this house. It's much more than just a roof over my head. I've tended the gardens for six years. Did you know Creggan took a first prize last year for my Madame Isaac Pereire?"

"I take it that's a flower, not a person?"

"An old rose, deep pink and very fragrant." She stepped to the window and pointed to a freshly dug bed. "Everything that grows on the estate has been nurtured. All the beds are double dug, and I fertilize and weed regularly. You won't find better soil in the county. Or lovelier flowers."

"The gardens may be lovely," he muttered, "but—"

"That's because I compost and cultivate to continually improve them." It was working! His face relaxed a bit as he gazed out the window. She'd get him to see things from her point of view, and then he'd let her stay. A bubble of relief rose in her chest.

He turned toward her and almost smiled.

At that moment her large orange cat strolled into the room and meowed.

April absent-mindedly petted the plump feline. "In a minute, Pumpkin."

She tossed McKittrick a sidelong glance. "There're also the cats." She had him now. She knew a cat person when she saw one.

"Cats?" He squinted warily at the animal. "How many cats?"

April hesitated. Did she dare tell him?

"How many cats?" he repeated.

"Nine."

"Good Lord!" He snorted and stared out the window once more.

Damn. How could she tell what he was thinking if he wouldn't look at her. "But they're mostly little ones!" she exclaimed. "They don't eat much and they catch mice and—"

"Nine cats," he muttered. "A flower-crazy woman and nine cats. Just what I need."

He spun from the window and faced her. "No."

"No what?" His unusual eyes had hardened into chunks of granite. Her heart began to sink.

"No cats. And no roses or wreaths or whatever it is you make. You've got thirty days."

Turning on his heel, he yanked open the door and stalked out into the rain.

TWO

Tom waded through a sea of oozy brown mud to get to his Mercedes. With each step, the rain-sodden ground sucked at his Bally loafers, covering the sides and tops in a layer of mud. Just what he needed, a thunderstorm on top of a one-hundred-mile drive to his grandfather's estate. And that after the longest, most grueling executive board meeting he'd ever conducted. He'd laid out his objections to the new corporate policy, listened to evasions and excuses until his temples pounded, then announced his resignation. That part felt good, at any rate.

And finally getting to Creggan and some badly needed peace and quiet—that felt good, too. It was a relief to finally be alone to sort out his options and put his life together. His corporate life, that is. His personal life was just the way he wanted it—unencumbered and uncomplicated.

But trying to talk sense to April Fairchild this afternoon had severely tilted his carefully balanced equilibrium.

He'd expected her to be gone by now. Why hadn't his

attorney evicted the woman on schedule? That was what he paid him for.

Tom slid into the driver's seat, dripping water on the grey leather. Had she really said nine cats? Unbelievable! He'd thought she'd be fortysomething and overweight. Instead she looked as young and slender as a high school girl. Even her forthright manner surprised him. Hell, he was learning a lot of unbelievable things lately.

He jammed the key in the ignition and listened to the throaty rumble of the engine over the splatter of rain. Just when he thought things were simple, they got complicated. Just when he had his company running the way he wanted, the tables turned, and he had nothing. No company. No job. And no damn idea what to do next. Except take it easy. That was what his doctor had ordered. He raked his fingers through the wet hair that flopped over his forehead. Getting heated up over his tenant was no way to lower his stress level. Dr. Martin had been explicit in his instructions. *Absolutely no stress.*

The downpour increased as the car jounced up the drive toward the main house. His house. A plume of brackish water sprayed over the left fender. "Damn." The car's fuel injection system was dicey when wet.

He pulled the Mercedes up to the house and sat for a moment, staring at it. He hadn't visited Creggan since high school, but the house looked the same—cream-colored stucco with half-timber trim and a massive river-rock chimney that extended up the two stories. As rustic as he'd remembered but still impressive.

He fingered the key his attorney had given him. Maybe it was a damn fool thing he'd done, putting his San Francisco condo on the market and coming back to the country for a rest. But after the Coastal Systems merger, he was bone tired and fed up. Before the ink was dry on the papers, their CEO had laid out his ideas to Tom and that was that. He couldn't stomach them. And after his bad EKG and Doc Martin's ultimatum, he'd been just plain scared.

He dashed through the rain and up the stone steps to the entry, fitted the key in the lock, and shoved the massive front door open. He stepped inside, groped for the light switch, and flipped it on.

Nothing.

"What the hell?" he muttered. Jim said he'd arrange for the power to be turned on. What had happened? The black chasm he knew was the foyer yawned before him.

Tom rubbed his arms and shivered. He'd been so flummoxed in the Fairchild woman's cottage, he'd stalked out and left his jacket on the chair. Better grab his flashlight and get a fire going.

Bracing himself, he dashed outside. Rain slashed his chest, soaking his shirt. He fumbled in the glove box for his flashlight and prayed the batteries weren't dead.

The interior of the house was as dark as midnight. He switched on the flashlight and followed the thin beam over to a section of walnut paneling, then moved the beam to a corner and paused. Cobwebs swathed the walls. God almighty, the spiders had taken over.

Something moved against his pantleg, and he jumped back. "Whoa!" Silence, then a tiny scratching noise skittered across the floor. Tom gritted his teeth. He liked his wildlife stuffed or on TV, not up close. City living was challenging enough.

He stomped his feet and a cloud of dust puffed beneath

his shoes. Flashing the beam into the open living room, he strode forward. Dingy sheets covered the furniture; newspapers littered the floor. One brown drape hung half torn from a wrought iron rod. Nearby sat a dilapidated cardboard box, half filled with kindling.

He jerked the light back to the pile of newspapers. Beside them was a dried glob of God knew what. By the look of things, no one had been in here in years. What the hell happened to the cleaning service Jim had arranged for? The room stank of mold and stale air.

He let out a weary breath. He remembered passing a seedy-looking motel about five miles back, but the NO VACANCY sign was lit. He'd have to make the best of it, but he'd call Jim this minute and chew him out.

He punched in his attorney's number. In seconds, the blinking NO SERVICE message popped up on the display. It figured. His phone must have faded out when he started up into the hills.

Tom surveyed the cavernous fireplace. At least he could get a fire started. He strode to the front door, wondering where they would have stacked that load of wood he'd ordered. The side yard?

The ground at the side of the house was bare except for a rusted, upturned wheelbarrow and a mound of river rocks. He strode around to the back. More rocks, a cracked flowerpot, and a burn barrel. Inside it were a few blackened madrone branches.

Damn it, nothing was going right. He yanked the largest piece out of the barrel and continued his search. There had to be some wood on the property. Trees surrounded the place, for chrissake. A fallen limb would do. No, he decided, eyeing the downpour. Too water-soaked.

Back at the front step, he scraped his shoes on the riser to get the mud off and tramped back into the living room. He pulled his microcassette out of his shirt pocket and began to dictate. "Check on wood delivery, call P.G. and E." Then he gathered up a fistful of the old newspapers, some shredded cardboard and a few sticks of kindling, and one chunk of madrone he'd found propped against the back door. After checking the chimney damper, he laid a fire, then touched a match to it. The kindling flared.

He watched the flames lick the madrone log. The knot of tension between his shoulder blades eased, and he rubbed his hands together in satisfaction. At last, something worked right.

In the next moment, smoke poured into the room.

"What the hell?" He bolted outside to check the chimney. No smoke. The damn chimney must be clogged. He raced inside, kicked the fire apart, and fanned the smoke away with a handful of newspaper pages. Then he crouched on his heels, lowered his head between his hands, and tried not to cough in the eye-stinging air.

No lights, no cleaning service, no wood, and a plugged chimney. So far, all his plans had bombed.

He thought of the annoying woman in the cottage with a gaggle of cats and her eucalyptus wreaths. Well, he'd solved that one—in thirty days she'd be gone.

His stomach growled. He hadn't eaten since breakfast, but the prospect of a can of cold tomato soup wasn't appealing. He thought of the New York strip steak he'd packed in his ice chest and groaned. No way to cook it.

Oh, hell, he might as well turn in. He didn't like sleeping in the house in its dilapidated state, but he'd had enough for one day. Tomorrow, he'd get someone in to fix the chimney.

He clicked on the flashlight and started down the hall toward his grandfather's room.

A yellowed sheet covered the double bed. He stripped it off and froze with it in his hand. Rats had built a nest in the center of the mattress. A tiny pair of eyes focused on him, then disappeared into a ragged hole surrounded by chunks of foam rubber.

"Jesus!" He turned on his heel and marched back into the foyer. He wouldn't spend another minute here until the cleaning crew and the exterminators went over every inch of the place. He whipped out his microcassette again. "Call cleanup service, exterminator. Order new bed, king-size." He switched it off and stuffed it back into his pocket.

The problem was what to do now.

April dried the coffee mugs and heated a pot of chicken soup. She had not planned to leave the cottage for another fourteen years. She'd assumed that even when the old man passed on, his heirs would let her stay. After all, she had a lease.

What happened now? She had never needed to give much thought to where she'd go from here. She hadn't counted on Tom McKittrick being such a jerk.

She sucked in a breath, let it out slowly. Well, not a jerk exactly, but he hadn't shown any sympathy for her situation.

She plopped a soup bowl onto the counter. "It isn't as if I'd be in your way," she muttered to herself. "I'm not

interested in seeing you any more than you want to see
me."

Shadow sat on the edge of the counter and blinked.

"I'm not talking to you," she addressed the cat. "I'm
just . . . talking. Getting it off my chest." Tomorrow
she'd have to try to make him agree to let her stay. The
thought of confronting him made her stomach clench.

Something banged against her door, and April started.
The cat leapt off the counter and scampered into the bedroom.

She sucked in a lungful of air. "Who's there?"

"McKittrick."

She cracked the open door. Tom McKittrick stood under the eave, dripping wet, and scowling. "Mrs. Fairchild,
I—I need help."

She let out the breath she was holding. Well, that was
a switch! "Come on in."

His mouth formed a grim line. "My plans went hay-
wire. There's no power, and the cleaning service didn't
show, and. . . ." He stared at her glass-fronted wood-
stove.

April noted his sodden shirt and handed him the towel
he'd used earlier. "You forgot your jacket."

With hands that shook, he wiped his hair and face. A
pool of muddy water formed by his feet. He looked down
at the mud and slipped out of his loafers. "Sorry," he
said in a tight voice.

"Sit down by the fire." She tried not to smile at the
picture he made—dripping wet silk shirt clinging to his
torso like a second skin, necktie limp and askew, unruly
hair plastered to his skull, and his expensive loafers
caked with mud.

He moved in front of the stove. "I ordered a cord of wood. It didn't arrive."

April pursed her lips. "John Malone's truck is in the shop for repairs, but even if it weren't, that wood wouldn't have done you any good. Swallows are nesting in your chimney."

He rolled his eyes. "It figures. Look, could I use your phone? I need to find a motel for the night. I can't stay at the house—rats have set up house in the mattress."

He looked so vulnerable she almost laughed. The city boy, out of place in the country. She crossed her arms over her midriff and inclined her head toward the kitchen counter. "Help yourself."

He pulled the directory from under the telephone, riffled the pages, and dialed.

"I need a room for the night. . . . Look, I'm not fussy. Anything will do. . . . Not until next Tuesday? I see." He purposefully placed the receiver in its cradle.

After a moment's silence, he spoke, his voice taut. "There aren't any other motels in town?"

April shook her head. "Just two. And they're always booked up this time of year."

Tom scowled.

She watched him thumb through more pages. Served him right. Deep down, she didn't want him to find Lupine Valley hospitable. Deep down she wanted him gone.

"I have a guest room," she heard herself say. "It's my workroom, but there's a fold-down bed."

He looked up, an odd expression on his face. "I need to find something in town."

She focused on his tie, a Versace original, she'd bet.

"It's up to you, but the nearest town is Santa Rosa, and it's forty miles away."

"My damned luck," he muttered. "Sorry, it's been a long day." The look on his face was more exasperated than apologetic, she decided.

His hair had begun to dry. She'd thought it a dark chestnut-brown, but now she could see the top layer was attractively silvered. He looked about thirty-five but was prematurely gray. His tumbled hair suited him.

"You haven't many choices, Mr. McKittrick."

He laid the towel over the chair back and searched her face. "You wouldn't mind?"

She quashed the niggle of uncertainty, made a bland face. "You're the landlord. Why should I mind?"

He jerked his gaze away. "I'll take my chances in town. Thanks anyway." He pulled his jacket off the back of the chair, shrugged into it, and marched out the door.

"Suit yourself," April said to his retreating figure. If he wanted to drive forty miles, it was his business.

Tom jammed his key in the ignition and started the engine. The tires spun a couple of times before he managed to move forward. In the short time he'd been in the cottage, the road had become a quagmire.

He made a hard left turn to avoid a pothole. Suddenly, the Mercedes listed to the left, and he felt the tires sink into the soft shoulder. The car lurched to a stop.

He revved the engine. The tires spun, but the car was firmly stuck in the mud. He pounded his fist on the steering wheel. That was all he needed! He could spend the night in the car or he could take his chances with the rats.

Gritting his teeth, he climbed out. Wet mud lapped over the tops of his shoes as he tramped around to open the trunk. He grabbed his flight bag in one hand, his flashlight in the other, and headed toward the main house.

He dropped the bag on the porch while he sifted through his pants pocket for the house key. A rock lodged itself under his right insole. His ankle bone, not fully recovered from last year's skiing accident, screamed with each step. He'd sell his soul right now for a hot bath and some dinner.

He shoved the key in the front door lock and gave it a turn. The head of the key came away in his hand.

He stared at the piece of metal in his palm. "Sweet Jesus. I don't believe this!" The shank had broken off in the lock. What in God's name was he going to do now?

April cut two slices of sourdough bread, laid a thick chunk of sharp cheddar on one, then covered it with the other slice and dropped it in a buttered skillet. When golden cheese melted out of the sandwich, she slid it onto a green plate and shoved slices of sweet pickle between the crusts. Her stomach rumbled as she ladled soup into a flat bowl and carried it to the kitchen table.

It was way past dinnertime, but she'd been distracted by Tom McKittrick and hadn't noticed how hungry she was. She shooed Pumpkin from her chair and settled into the padded seat.

She spooned a mouthful of soup. Tom McKittrick was a strange man. He'd obviously wanted to warm himself by her fire, but he'd been uncomfortable around her. If she didn't know better, she'd say his conscience was bothering him. But men like him didn't have consciences, she reminded herself. Men like Tom McKittrick made the world run to suit themselves and to hell with anybody else.

The soup was just right—chickeny and redolent with thyme and lemon, just like they served in the Greek restaurant in town. The perfect supper for a rainy night. She might have shared some with McKittrick. She had no sympathy for his method of business, but he'd looked so pathetic with his soggy shoes and clothes that a part of her wanted to reach out to him. The other part held steadfast. He didn't need a nursemaid; he could take care of himself.

A loud rap on the door jarred her. What now? She rose and peered out the peephole.

On the other side of the door stood Tom McKittrick, his jacket a limp ruin of the expensive suede she'd admired earlier, a leather flight bag clutched in one hand. One glimpse of the desperate look on his face and her resolve melted. She opened the door and stepped aside.

He stalked in.

She met his gaze and pointed to her workshop. Without a word, he strode past her.

Five minutes later, he still hadn't emerged. Well, she couldn't just ignore him. She'd bet he hadn't eaten.

She knocked on his door. "Are you hungry?"

He stared at her across the threshold, toothbrush in hand. "Yeah, starving."

"How about chicken soup and a grilled cheese sandwich?"

He closed his eyes for an instant, apparently wrestling with the idea. April waited. How long did it take to decide whether or not to eat? "Oh, well, I just thought. . . ." She started back to the kitchen.

"I'd like that, Mrs. Fairchild. I'd like that very much."

April looked over her shoulder. "Dinner's in ten minutes."

McKittrick took two steps forward, his lean figure framed in the doorway. "Those are beautiful words, Mrs. Fairchild."

From the hallway, April spun around to face him and laughed. "Enjoy it while you can." She couldn't resist adding, "It only lasts thirty days."

THREE

Tom McKittrick slanted her a grin. "I suppose I deserve that."

April placed her hands on her hips. "Yes, as a matter of fact, you do."

Closing the space between them, he gazed down on her with dark, probing eyes. "Maybe. But it won't change anything."

April steadied herself, then fled to the kitchen.

He sat down at the antique, red lacquered table while she dished up a bowl of soup and set it in front of him. How did she approach a man who made her angry and vulnerable at the same time? With shaking hands, she slid the grilled cheese sandwich onto a plate. Then after taking a fortifying breath, she set it beside the soup and took the chair opposite him.

He balanced his spoon in long, manicured fingers. The man wasn't so much handsome as sexy, April decided. His eyes were a rich mahogany-flecked green. Arresting eyes that seemed to see everything. His gaze moved around the room, assessing, categorizing. He was probably the type of person who analyzed people and filed them in neat little boxes and never bothered to notice them as individuals. Corporate executives were like that. And he was definitely the CEO type. A suit.

He hesitated a moment, then met her gaze. Did he resent being studied? She gave him a tight smile and focused on the soup.

He brought the spoon to his lips. "I'm trying to think of what to say."

The silence hummed. He glanced at her briefly, then his gaze darted away.

She watched his fingers. "You could say the soup is good."

His jaw tensed. "The soup is excellent. That's not what I meant."

So much for levity. "You don't like being here, do you?"

He stared at the hand-crocheted tablecloth for a long moment. "Nothing has gone according to plan. The house is uninhabitable. You know a Thompson's Cleaning Service?"

She raised her eyes. "Lupine Valley is a small town, Mr. McKittrick."

He bit into the grilled cheese and chewed impatiently. "They're damned inefficient."

April set her spoon down on the plate. "Dave Thompson fell off his pickup and broke his elbow."

"That's no excuse. Does he work alone?"

"His son helps him, but he's in Sacramento for the state science fair." She chewed on her lower lip. "You're desperate to move in right away?"

He flashed her a sharp-eyed look. "Not with no heat, no lights, no—"

"Yes, you said you had no power. Did you check the fuse box?"

His face changed. "No. Should I have?"

April hid her astonishment behind a smile. "Mr. McKittrick, you're obviously not a country boy. Things are different here; we don't take things much for granted. Like old wiring and fuse boxes."

"I'm beginning to see that." He drummed his fingers on the tabletop, then paused and dropped his hand in his lap. "Look, you know the town. If you could just recommend a good handyman, I'll try to. . . ."

She knew he was uncomfortable, out of his element in the country. And obviously ill at ease in her cottage. Desperation must have driven him back to her door. "Mr. McKittrick, would you like some coffee?"

Seconds ticked by. He drew in a slow breath, let it out. "No. Yes." She noted the flare of something undefinable in his eyes.

She pushed back her chair, stepped to the coffee mill and poured in a handful of shiny black beans, sensing that he watched her. While the machine whirred, she switched on the kettle and fitted a glass filter over a green mug. Resisting the urge to glance surreptitiously at him, she spooned ground coffee into the filter paper and poured boiling water over it.

She looked up, their eyes met and held briefly. Her pulse gave an odd little leap, and she turned back to the coffee. She didn't want to find him attractive, but she did.

When the coffee finished dripping, she handed him the mug and a pitcher of cream and led the way to the living room.

"Where's yours?"

"I don't drink coffee at night," she said in a clipped tone. Sharing coffee with Tom McKittrick seemed too friendly; she didn't want to have any feelings whatsoever for this man.

He lowered himself onto one end of the sofa, warily eyeing Pumpkin, who occupied the opposite corner. Shadow, draped around the woodstove, peered at Tom through slitted eyes. Sally, her small mackerel tabby, materialized from under the overstuffed chair and rubbed against Tom's leg. He pulled away, a flicker of annoyance crossing his face. Her original assessment that he liked cats was incorrect; Tom McKittrick didn't like cats.

He took a sip from the mug. "Nine cats, huh? Seems like a lot."

She sat down in the easy chair, smoothed her palms over the knees of her jeans, and made room for Sally. "They had no place else to go." She scratched Sally's ear. "I manage to find homes for a few, but others always turn up."

He frowned at the cat, then brought his gaze to the books. "You have a lot of books, too."

She stilled her hand. "I brought them from home."

"Oh?" Again that light flickered in his eyes. "Where's home?"

She pressed her lips together, kept her hands curved around Sally's soft fur. "Until yesterday, I thought it was right here."

His eyes darkened. He set his mug on the coffee table. "I believe I've made myself clear on that."

"Quite clear, Mr. McKittrick. I just don't understand why. Your grandfather—"

"There's nothing to understand. I'm the owner, and I simply want to be alone. The last month has been . . . difficult."

"Lupine Valley is a long way from San Francisco. Not many people want to make that commute."

His brows lowered. "Nor do I. I won't be going to the city."

April's jaw dropped, and she immediately clamped her lips together. "You won't? Isn't your office in San Francisco?"

"Not any more. I've decided to try country living." He unfolded himself from the sofa and took a step toward the pine shelves lining one wall of the room, then faced her. "I can see that staying at Creggan is important to you, however. . . ."

April's hand stilled on the cat's fur. "It's a refuge, Mr. McKittrick. I'm at peace here."

"Do you do all the maintenance yourself?"

"You mean cutting wood and hauling fallen limbs? Yes. I do it all myself."

He pulled a book from the shelf, examined it and put it back. "I suppose you were used to country life before?"

Her thoughts shifted to the Massachusetts town house she had shared with Teddy. "No, I lived in a medium-size town. When I was married, we had hired help. Now, out here, everything I do I've had to learn myself."

He digested this, then turned to scan the books once more. He paused to stare at the photograph. "This man looks familiar—I'm sure I've seen him before."

"He was my husband. He was well-known."

"Fairchild? That's it! Teddy Fairchild." He swung around "Wasn't he . . . ?"

"Teddy was killed at Monaco."

He ran a finger over the silver frame. "I remember that race. His car slammed into the wall. The newspapers said he'd have won if he hadn't crashed."

April clamped her teeth together. "Well, people say a lot of things. The fact is, he did crash, and he's dead."

She set the cat aside and rose. She didn't like to think about it. Not then, not now. "I have work to do early tomorrow, so I'll do up the dishes and turn in. If you don't want cats on your bed, close the door." She moved toward the kitchen sink.

Tom looked down at the two felines at his feet. Useless pieces of fur. April didn't appear to mind them in the least. Well, April Fairchild was different.

He studied her backside. She was unlike anyone he'd met before. Her eyes were a pale silvery blue, almost transparent, and they really got to him. He let his gaze wander over her slender, jean-clad form. Long legs, narrow hips, small, high breasts. And that blond hair, the color of wheat. She seemed unaware of her attractiveness, but her body made his pulse pound.

He rose, placed his mug on the counter, and headed toward his room. The fold-down bed seemed impossibly small, but it would do for tonight. He gazed at the pine chest of drawers on one wall, the row of windows above a built-in counter. Baskets of dried flowers, jars of herbs, and piles of leaves mounded in terra-cotta pots sat neatly in one corner. Rolls of ribbon and twine hung from pegs above them.

The work space suited her, he decided. Neat and tidy.

He just couldn't imagine what she did with all her herbs and ribbons.

Through the open door, he watched her washing dishes, her hands buried in a mound of soapsuds. She looked the picture of domesticity, and as female as hell. He could guess why his grandfather had allowed her to stay.

She didn't want him here, he knew that right away. But she was hospitable, and he liked that. And she had one other thing—something he'd lost along the corporate trail. Compassion. He liked that about her, too.

As a matter of fact, he liked a lot of things about her. He reached into his flight bag and took out his toilet articles.

Part of him was glad Teddy Fairchild was dead, that she didn't have a husband. Another part—deep in his gut—felt a knot of fear. She was beautiful . . . and different.

He knew how to deal with attractive women—dinner, the opera, maybe a nightclub. Sex. That part came easy. But April Fairchild wasn't like those women. Something about her touched his core, tugged at longings he'd thought buried.

Tom pressed his palms to his head. The dull ache behind his temples during dinner had turned into a roaring headache. Each movement felt as though a jackhammer were chinking out bits of his skull.

He glanced toward the kitchen where April wiped the counter with a white dishcloth. "Do you have any aspirin?"

"Yes," she responded without turning. "I'll put it out on the counter."

Tom made his way into the bathroom, showered, and brushed his teeth. Then he slipped on a pair of burgundy silk pajama bottoms and his jacquard dressing gown and strode into the kitchen. Each step intensified the relentless ache behind his eyes.

April was gone, but a blue-and-white capsule lay on the white Formica. He grabbed a glass from the cabinet, filled it, and downed the capsule. Kick in quick, he prayed.

She walked in, the orange cat under one arm, a small bottle clutched in her free hand. "Here's your aspirin."

"I just took the one you laid out."

Her eyes rounded. "You . . . took the capsule on the counter?"

"Sure. It was right there where you said it would be."

Her lips twitched. She set the cat on the floor, put a hand to her mouth. Her laughter bubbled up like water purling over rocks.

"What's so funny?"

Tears formed at the corners of her eyes. She brushed them away and held out her hand. "The aspirin's right here. That capsule was for Pumpkin."

He clapped a hand to his throat. "You mean I took cat medicine? What the hell kind?"

"Pumpkin has an irregularity problem," she said between hiccups of laughter. "I give her Vetamucil. Metamucil for cats."

"Jesus." He pressed his fingers between his eyes.

She tried unsuccessfully to wipe the smile off her face, then gave up. "Don't worry, Mr. McKittrick. It won't have any effect on anyone weighing over ten pounds."

"Metamucil for cats. I'll be damned."

He took the bottle from her, shook out three tablets, and swallowed them with the remaining water. Giving April an exasperated look, he strode toward his room.

April watched his pajama-clad back disappear into her workroom. For an uptight CEO with a chip on his executive shoulder, he wasn't too bad. She suppressed a giggle. Three aspirin and a Vetamucil. He ought to sleep like a hibernating bear.

"Good night, Mr. McKittrick."

"Oh, hell, call me Tom."

FOUR

Tom awoke to the smell of frying bacon, coffee, and a weight on his ankles. He tried wiggling one toe. No good. His foot was immobilized.

He raised one eyelid, peered at the end of the bed. Three cats sprawled over his feet as if they owned the place. He opened both eyes. Now he remembered; he'd spent the night in April Fairchild's workshop.

A slit of light shone through the door. He must have forgotten to shut it completely, and now her damned cats had taken over the bed. He studied the orange mound draped over his left foot. Pancake or some such name. "Shoo. Scram."

The cat gave him a languid stare, then began to wash one ginger-colored paw.

He pulled himself to a sitting position, eyeing the animals. Then he swung his legs over the side of the narrow bed, got to his feet, and stretched. Amazing what Vetamucil, aspirin, and a night's sleep could do for a man.

A ray of sunlight peeked through the chintz curtains. A good sign; the rain had let up. Today, he would accomplish some things.

April turned when Tom McKittrick stepped into the kitchen. Shaved and showered, his hair still damp, he looked handsome in tan corduroy trousers and a soft-looking cream cashmere pullover. What he didn't look like was a man about to embark on heavy-duty house-cleaning.

She glanced at her worn jeans and thrift shop flannel shirt with the frayed tail and bit back a giggle. Mr. City Mouse probably didn't even own a pair of Levi's or a work shirt.

And he certainly didn't look at home.

She handed him a coffee mug. "Good morning. Coffee's on the stove; cream's on the table. Did you sleep well?" She swung back to the stove, feeling his eyes on her.

"Fair. The cats decided they had squatters' rights."

"Pumpkin. She's the instigator—the others follow. They're like the three musketeers." She lifted bacon strips onto a plate, cracked two eggs in the skillet, and punched down the toaster. "We got six inches of rain last night. Worst spring storm in twenty years."

Tom filled his cup, ignored the cream, then lowered his frame into the chair. "Today I'm going to get someone to clean out the chimney, maybe give Thompson a call."

April slid two fried eggs onto the plate and set it on the table, then poured herself a cup of coffee. She didn't want to care. Anything she did to make things easier would shorten her future at the cottage. But she knew exactly how he felt. Six years ago when she first came up here, she'd needed all the help she could get.

"Dave Thompson's arm's still in a cast," she said

against her better judgment. "But I have a friend who's good with chimneys."

"I need help getting my car out of the mud, too."

"Raven has a four-wheel-drive truck."

"Raven?" He stared at her. "The man's name is Raven?"

"Funny name. Big heart."

Tom studied his breakfast, then looked up. "Give him a call."

Tom eyed the mud-washed lane, listened for the sound of a truck engine, then went back for a second box of newspapers. He'd swept out the living room and hauled the mattress and cartons of junk onto the porch. He was tired and cold and his clothes were filthy. If April's friend would just show up, he could at least get some heat.

He spied her in the side yard that ran from his house to her cottage, moving from shrub to shrub, spreading stuff around the base of each plant. Fertilizer, he guessed. Down on her knees with her back to him she presented a fine view of her rounded derriere.

She stood up and stretched, her red shirt pulling against firm, high breasts. Aware of a tightening in his groin, he rimmed his lower lip with his tongue. He hadn't been with a woman for so long, he'd almost forgotten the pull. These past four months he'd been so busy getting ready for the merger and the annual stockholders meeting that he hadn't had time.

Maybe it was just as well. He was never sure whether a woman was interested in him or his power to make money. What he needed was. . . .

Oh, hell, if he knew what he needed, he wouldn't be here waiting for a chimney sweep and trying to figure out his life.

He lifted the cardboard box in his arms and eyed the wheat-colored hair April had tied back with a red scarf. The ends fell like spun silk on her shoulders. He rested the carton on his knee and stared at her. He wanted to sift that hair through his fingers, press his mouth against it. He closed his eyes. Her hair would smell of flowers.

Get a grip, McKittrick. He needed to stop daydreaming and get his house in order.

He dragged his gaze back to the carton in his arms, ordered his feet down the steps, and strode to the pile of discarded stuff in the driveway. Tom stared down the empty lane. Ten-thirty and still no sign of April's friend. What the hell kind of hours did the guy keep?

He couldn't go to Santa Rosa without his car, but if he didn't get there and buy a bed, he'd have nothing to sleep on. Gritting his teeth, he snatched the broom and began to sweep out the bedroom. Dust swirled into his eyes.

Another hour went by. Tom surveyed his dirt-smudged sweater and swore aloud. Things sure moved slowly in the country!

Finally he heard the whine of a car and strode to the front door to see a dark-green pickup of uncertain vintage clatter up the drive. A lanky young man hopped out. Long, ginger-colored ponytail tied with a cord, a wispy beard, a couple of turquoise bead necklaces, and an ankh on a length of rawhide around his throat. Black T-shirt, tie-dyed drawstring trousers.

Tom let out a gust of air. Out in the sticks, beggars

weren't choosers. This kid was going to help him get his car unstuck and his fireplace working.

"Yo, April," the man called. He wandered toward the shrubs and pulled April into an embrace. Tom noted that he held her for what seemed a very, very long minute. Just when he felt his hands clench, the kid released her.

What the hell kind of "friend" was this guy? Tom clamped a lid on his annoyance and stepped onto the porch as April motioned the ponytail toward the house.

The man bounded up the steps, a thin hand thrust forward. "McKittrick? I'm Raven, friend of April's." He turned to give her a smile. Too warm a smile, Tom decided.

"So, you need the chimney cleaned?"

"I also need my car pulled out of the ditch," Tom said, his voice gruff.

"That your Mercedes blocking April's driveway?" Raven whistled. "Nice wheels."

Tom scowled. "Maybe not so nice. The left front wheel is buried up to the axle."

"That's a hauling machine," Raven murmured, scratching his head. "You don't see many 600 class coupes out here. Must've set you back a few pennies."

Tom hid his surprise. The young man looked more like his specialty ran to psychedelic-painted Volkswagen vans. "I buy for performance. Look, can you pull it out before you start on the chimney? I need to get to Santa Rosa."

The kid eyed him for a long moment, then shoved his hands in his pockets. "Piece of cake, man. We'll dig under the wheels and shore up with some two-by-twelves." He called to April who was gathering her tools and bucket in the side yard. "You still got those boards out behind your place, babe?"

Babe? He calls her babe? What does she call him? he wondered. *Oh, forget it, McKittrick.* What they said to each other was none of his business.

She called out from the circle of shrubs, a few feet away. "I used a couple for a raised dahlia bed, but there're plenty behind the house. Help yourself. I'm going inside to finish my Tuesday orders."

"I'll get started in a mo," Raven answered, moving toward his truck. "I want to check out the chimney first."

"But—" Tom began.

"Relax, buddy. Ol' Raven'll fix you up. Not to worry." He ambled over to his vehicle and pulled an aluminum ladder off the rack.

Tom propped his hands on his hips and stared first at the gangly handyman, then at April Fairchild's trim backside as she walked across the meadow to her cottage. He felt like the odd man out. What the hell was he supposed to do while Rogaine or whatever his name was puttered in his chimney?

He stalked into the house, grabbed the broom he'd left lying in a corner of the living room, and began brushing the cobwebs that clung to the walls. Within ten minutes the lanky handyman appeared, shaking his head. "No way am I gonna clean your chimney now, man. There's eggs in that nest."

Tom blinked. "Eggs? What's that got to do with anything?"

The younger man pinned him with deep-set eyes. "You gotta respect the birds—they got rights, too. Those eggs are gonna hatch any day now. But tell you what"—his serious look melted in a spontaneous grin—"as soon as they leave the nest I'll come back and take care of it for ya."

Tom groaned. "How long will that take?"

Raven cocked his head to one side. "Oh, an hour or so."

"I mean," Tom bit the words out, "how long until the eggs hatch and the birds fly out and I can use my chimney?" He glared at the young man.

Raven passed off his remark with a chuckle. "Four, maybe five weeks."

Tom groaned. "Four weeks." At least it wasn't the dead of winter. "Now about my car—"

Raven secured the ladder on the truck rack, then stepped to the driver's side and opened the door. "See ya later."

Tom jerked. "What do you mean, later? My car—"

Raven shrugged. "I promised a man some wood. Gotta deliver it now. I'll be back in a bit." He hopped into the driver's seat. The truck roared to life and rolled down the driveway.

"God almighty." Tom pounded his fist on his thigh. If Raven wouldn't stick around to do the job, he'd do it himself. It didn't sound all that difficult. He strode across the meadow and pounded on April's front door.

She opened it just enough to peer out. Her "what now?" look made his jaw tighten. He hated to ask for help.

"I need a shovel."

She hesitated.

"For the car," he added.

"Around the back." She closed the door in his face.

He found the shovel, carried it over to his Mercedes, then went back for the boards. He loaded two of them onto his shoulder, and plodded toward the mired vehicle. He tipped one shoulder, slid the boards to the ground, and yanked his hand back. A splinter stabbed into the crease of his left thumb.

Favoring his left hand, he dug the mud out from behind each tire and shoved a board under the front wheels. When he straightened, a muscle spasm ripped his lower back. Both palms were blistered, and mud caked his cords from the knees down.

He shrugged his watch from under the sleeve of his filthy sweater. Four-thirty. Another hour and the stores in Santa Rosa would close.

Climbing into the driver's seat, he gingerly laid one hand on the steering wheel, and switched on the ignition.

From the kitchen window, April watched him rev the engine, watched the tires spin in the mud. She gritted her teeth. Part of her wanted him to fail, but she needed to deliver six wreaths and a dozen packets of lavender sachet to Rosie's and he was blocking the driveway. Rosie paid on delivery, and April needed the money to cover the check she'd written the day before.

April sighed. Usually her problems came one at a time, and she could handle them the same way, but the last twenty-four hours had pushed all her buttons. For six years she'd barely managed to survive, and now two things were clear: One, she was not ready to move. And two, without a windfall, her herb business would go under.

"Face it, girl, you're going to starve by summer if sales don't pick up."

The left rear tire of the Mercedes settled deeper into the mud and spun to a stop. April bit her lip. Should she go out to help him? If she could catch Rosie before she left her shop, it would be worth it, but on the other hand, watching the rich city executive struggle with the elements was entertaining, especially seeing him mess up his expensive sweater and trousers.

Her chest tightened. She hadn't felt this detached since Teddy died. When had she turned so callous?

All right, she *would* give McKittrick a hand. But she'd ask for something in return. She'd insist he give her an hour of his undivided attention, and she'd talk straight to him about letting her stay.

She pushed her feet into the Wellingtons she kept by the back door, marched outside, and tapped on the car window. "You need some weight behind it."

Tom rolled down the window. "Got any suggestions?"

"Let me push."

"If anyone pushes it'll be me."

"Suit yourself. I'll drive. *You* push."

Tom frowned, but he shoved open the door and climbed out.

April slipped behind the wheel, put the car into reverse, and watched Tom through the windshield as he leaned against the bumper. Then she tapped the accelerator.

The tires spun, and mud sprayed Tom from his hair to his fancy loafers. He swore and shoved his weight against the hood.

April shoved her foot down on the accelerator, and slowly the car began to move. The engine whined, the tires shot up onto the boards, and the vehicle spurted onto the driveway.

Tom stumbled around to the driver's side, wiping his face on his sleeve. "Thanks for the help," he said in a tight voice. Mud flecks stuck to his hair.

"No problem. You were blocking the driveway. Quick, what time is it?"

"Five o'clock."

She squeezed her eyelids closed. "Too late."

"For me, too. I wanted to buy a bed." He pulled a handkerchief from his pocket and wiped a blob of mud clinging to his forehead. "Guess I'll have to use your phone."

April focused on the square line of his jaw, the straight, mud-smeared nose. "Help yourself. Then I'd like to talk to you."

Trembling, April stopped at the door and shed her boots. She didn't want him in her house, didn't want to face him, but she had to talk, and this seemed the best time to get him to listen to her. She gave him a pointed look, then stepped inside. Tom met her gaze, then looked down at his own feet. Bending, he slipped off his muddy loafers.

She watched him thumb through the yellow pages, then dial.

"I want a bed delivered immediately. . . . I don't know which one. King-size. Firm mattress. . . . No, I haven't. . . . Yes. Yes. Just pick out one, deliver it right away." He let out a weary breath. "McKittrick at Creggan Estate in Lupine Valley. That's right."

He rolled his eyes. "Not until . . . Jesus. All right, tomorrow. And two down pillows, sheets, white ones, and a down comforter. . . . That's right." He recited a credit card number and hung up.

April stared at him. "You ordered a bed without trying it out?"

"What would you do?" he growled.

"I'd—why, I don't know. I was going to say, 'Stay in my workroom,' but—"

"But you don't really want me there."

"No," she said quietly. "I don't. But not for the reason you think."

He clenched and unclenched his fist. "Look, I didn't ask for this situation, and I sure as hell didn't expect to. . . ." He broke off. "I'm sorry about blocking your driveway. I'll make it up to you some way."

"I don't want—" *What did he say?* April suppressed a smile. *He'd make it up to her?* Good. She needed to talk to him about her lease, but he was always too busy. Now he owed her a favor and she had *him* over a barrel.

Tom started for the door. "Thanks for the use of your phone."

"But—but you said. . . ."

He gave her a harried look. "It'll have to wait. Right now, I've got to finish scrubbing the walls while I still have light."

The sun hung low on the horizon when Tom dumped his fourteenth bucket of dirty water off the front porch. After scouring dingy walls and the filthy floor in four upstairs rooms, his hands looked like two prunes, and his thumb with the splinter in it throbbed. His shoulder muscles screamed every time he picked up the broom.

But the bedroom and living room were spiderless. To-morrow, if he could still move two out of four of his limbs, he'd tackle the kitchen.

A vehicle rumbled up the driveway, and he set the bucket on the kitchen counter and limped back to the front door. Raven was unloading wood from his truck bed.

"Yo, Tom," he called. "I had extra. Figured you could use some for when you get your chimney working."

"Yeah. Well, thanks."

Raven shoved a log onto the ground. "I see you got your car out. Sorry 'bout not getting back earlier, ran into a problem."

He rolled the last of the wood off the truck, hopped down, and secured the tailgate. "I'll be back in the morning."

"Tomorrow," Tom muttered to the retreating truck. "I won't hold my breath." He turned toward the house and blew out a sigh. Now he faced that pile of wood that needed stacking. What he really felt like doing was having a long soak in a hot bath, but the wood had to be stacked.

He focused on the tower of split oak and madrone, and his entire body screamed, "Enough." But his grandfather's words echoed in his mind. *Do as much as you can, while you can.* The old man had taught him well. That philosophy had made Tom's company triple its stock value.

Actually, he figured stacking wood couldn't be any worse than scrubbing floors or walls.

* * *

April draped the damp dish towel over the rack near the sink. She still wasn't sure why she'd helped Tom get his car out of the mud. True, he'd made a pitiful sight in his dirt-streaked cashmere sweater and corduroys, but that wasn't the entire reason. There was something else, and that "something else" bothered her. She didn't want to feel anything for this man. Not pity, and certainly not "something else."

Off and on all afternoon she had observed him tossing buckets of dirty mop water off the front porch. She'd bet he'd never cleaned a house in his life, much less one as neglected as his grandfather's. Now, as she stared out the kitchen window, he worked in the fading light stacking the wood Raven had dumped in the yard. She'd say this for him, he might not be used to working with his hands, but he was certainly no slouch.

She grimaced as the woodpile grew. He was going about it all wrong. He should be crisscrossing the rows to allow the wood to dry out, and—more important—to keep the pile stable.

As she watched, one log rolled off the top of the stack onto the ground. Tom bent to retrieve it, and just at that moment another tumbled down, smacking right on top of his loafer.

April winced. *Oh, the poor, dumb . . . bastard.* She gripped the edge of the counter, a tingling sensation in her own toe. The trouble with type A males was they didn't know when to quit.

Tom danced around on one foot, in obvious pain, and she watched until she couldn't stand it any longer. Then she sighed, reached in a drawer for her work gloves, and started across the meadow.

FIVE

Tom leaned against the spreading tree next to the porch and massaged his throbbing foot. Damn it all! He should have left the wood stacking until tomorrow. He'd reached his limit hours ago, and all it had taken to push him over the edge was one lousy piece of firewood.

He fingered the knot on his instep and groaned. Maybe he wouldn't be able to walk tomorrow. He looked up to see April striding toward him, a distressed look on her face.

She jabbed her forefinger at his woodpile. "You're stacking the wood all wrong. It'll topple over like that."

"It already has."

"What you need—"

"What I need, Mrs. Fairchild," he got out through clenched teeth, "is to be left in peace."

She gazed at him a long moment, then marched over to the woodpile. She laid down a short row of logs, then chunked a new layer on top, turned ninety degrees. She reached for another log before he realized what she was doing.

"Hold it right there."

She met his gaze with raised eyebrows. "I thought I'd give you a hand."

Tom forced his shoe back on his aching foot and limped over to the woodpile. "Thanks for your advice, but I'll take care of it my way."

She dropped the log she was holding and faced him with her hands on her hips. "Okay, Mr. Executive, you do that. And when that pile comes tumbling down, remember I warned you." She spun and marched back toward her cottage. Tom stared at her retreating figure and couldn't help grinning. Pretty feisty for a slip of a woman.

The moment he put his weight on his injured foot, his smile faded. No good. He pushed the mop of hair off his forehead and glared at the woodpile. Beaten by something with no IQ at all.

He'd have to get Raven to stack it tomorrow. On second thought, given the ponytail's work habits, he probably wouldn't show up until noon. April apparently didn't share her friend's country ethic. She'd been on the go since dawn. That, and the way she'd kept up the estate grounds, impressed him. But it made no difference. He preferred to go it alone.

Tom eyed the ice chest he'd set on his front porch. The thought of a rare hunk of beef and a bottle of wine cheered his drooping spirits. At least he could enjoy a grilled steak for dinner tonight. His mouth watering, he set out for the house.

Wait a minute. The grill he remembered seeing was the barbecue cooker in April's yard. *Jesus!*

He stumbled up onto his porch, sank down on the first

step, and put his head between his hands. He hadn't felt this helpless since his first day in boot camp.

Okay, Tom. Decision time. He had two choices: He could drive to Santa Rosa or he could tough it out on his living room floor. Neither prospect sparked his interest. That left only one other possibility.

He stared at the light in the cottage window. With a sigh of resignation, he struggled to his feet, climbed the steps, and unsnapped the ice chest lid.

April shrugged out of her boots at her back step, stormed into the cottage, and slammed the door behind her. Well, Mr. City Boy could just simmer in his own broth for all she cared.

She opened the cupboard, snatched three cans of cat tuna off the shelf, and slapped them on the counter. Left his company, did he? Any man that pigheaded would be impossible to work for. He probably did his employees a favor by leaving.

She dished chunks of fish into three earthenware bowls. Four pair of eyes stared expectantly at the counter. A blue-eyed Siamese scolded in a raspy voice.

"I don't need your lip, either," she snapped. She placed one dish on the floor beside the cabinet and watched four heads merge around it. Cats do it; why can't people share as well?

Why am I so angry? He was just a stubborn man who happened to own the cottage she lived in. No reason to go ballistic. She drew in a shaky breath. Then why was her heart pounding like a trip-hammer? She stalked to the back door with the other two dishes and called to the other five cats. "Come and get it."

So, Mr. Independence thinks he can manage on his own, does he? Well, he was in for a surprise. In the country, people helped each other. If it hadn't been for neighbors and friends like Raven, she'd never have made it on her own.

She peered in the refrigerator for salad greens and the leftover soup. One way or another, Tom McKittrick had a lesson coming to him.

A knock rattled the front door. April set the bag of fresh-picked lettuce on the counter and opened the door. Tom stood rooted to the spot, a plastic-wrapped sirloin steak clutched in one outstretched hand.

A peace offering? She glanced at his tight-jawed face and swung the door wide.

He stalked in, slapped the meat down on her counter, and faced her. "Dinner in exchange for a bed?"

She knew those words cost him. She studied him, gathering her thoughts.

"I'll cook it," he added. "Just show me the grill."

April sighed. He looked done in. Mud encrusted his clothes. His thumb was bandaged, his right foot bulged out of his shoe. Here was a man who needed help. And, she thought with an odd spurt of glee, he needed it from her.

At last, she had him right where she wanted him—up to his tail feathers in alligators. She squashed down a surge of elation. Now was the time. If she played her cards right, she could name her own price.

"I have a better proposition. You get the bed and a

bath, and I cook the steak. In exchange, you give me one hour of your undivided attention. Deal?"

Tom expelled a slow breath. "Deal."

April avoided his gaze. It was one thing to beat a man at his own game, but she'd no time to gloat. Besides, his obvious discomfort made her throat tighten. "A soak in a hot bath does wonders for sore muscles."

"That would help," he admitted. "But the way my shoulders feel, I need a miracle."

"Green jar above the tub. Pour a capful in the water, soak for twenty minutes, and you'll feel like a new man."

"Sounds good. What's in it?"

"Salt crystals, rosemary, and lavender."

He wrinkled his nose. "Leaves and twigs, huh?"

Her mouth thinned. "My special formula."

She reached in the cupboard for her wooden salad bowl, set it on the counter, and faced him. "Don't analyze it, just try it."

Tom cast her a pensive look, then wheeled around and strode down the hall.

April tore lettuce into the bowl, then halved six cherry tomatoes and added them with one sliced green onion, all too aware of the splashing water filling her claw-foot bathtub. She set the bowl aside and marched outside to light the grill.

Moonlight filtered through the redwoods behind her cottage, the trees casting long shadows on the ground. The *hoo hoo hoo* of a horned owl broke the stillness. Ordinarily she would search the trees for its roost, but tonight she fixed her gaze on the shingled cottage wall behind the grill. On the other side of that wall, Tom

McKittrick's naked body soaked in her tub. She tried not to think about it.

While the coals burned to a cherry color, she rehearsed what she'd say to him when she got the chance. After he'd enjoyed his bath and the steak, they'd have coffee in the living room, and she'd make it clear about the lease. He had to be sympathetic; a good meal and coffee by the fire brought out the best in a person.

April's hand froze over the grill. She wasn't sure she *wanted* to see Tom McKittrick at his best. At his worst—weary and mud-spattered—he was a very sexy man. Just standing beside him made her nerve endings feel like they'd developed antennae.

She closed her eyes. She didn't want that feeling. She'd done without a man in her life for six years, and she planned to keep it that way. She felt safer with no emotional involvement.

But, she acknowledged, one man—the one in her bathtub—posed a threat. And that presented another problem.

She was sure she could get him to see things her way, let her stay on indefinitely. He couldn't be mulish if she was calm and rational in her presentation of the situation. No, a man as sensible as Tom McKittrick would soon see that having her here on the property was an asset.

The problem was, could she stand to be around *him?*

She stepped inside and grabbed the steak. When she laid the thick sirloin on the grill, the sizzle made her mouth water. It had been a long time since she'd eaten steak; she'd forgotten how good it smelled cooking. Reluctantly, she marched inside to steam the asparagus she'd bought at the farmers' market.

Tom dried himself off and slipped into his dark-green

jogging suit, the only thing in his wardrobe that didn't need a tie. He'd remedy that tomorrow. Out here, a man needed jeans and boots. He'd learned that quick enough.

He wiggled his toes into his right shoe. The knot on the top of his instep was the size of a champagne cork and hurt like the devil. He decided on just his socks.

"Dinner in five minutes," April called from the kitchen.

Tom ran his fingers through his hair and glanced at his face. The mud was gone and he had no bruises. He raised his arms and stretched in front of the mirror.

Damned if she wasn't right about those herbs. His shoulder muscles felt good enough for a set of tennis. In fact, he was ready to sample that steak.

In the mirror he saw a shelf with more bottles. Lotions, powders, liquids in green and frosted glass. He uncorked one and sniffed. Whatever it was smelled like geraniums. Nice. In fact, the entire cottage was unique. Like her.

He imagined her bedroom would be similar, a flowered quilt, plump pillows. Nothing fancy, or overruffled, just comfortable.

For a long moment he stood still while an unexpected yearning for something he couldn't name washed over him.

He lifted a maple hand mirror from the white painted chest beside the washstand, felt the smooth, rubbed wood. Everything, the fluffy, yellow towels hanging on the rack, the tortoiseshell comb and brush, small glazed pots of lotion, looked inviting. A man could tell by looking around the cottage that April Fairchild was complex and creative. One look at her and he could also tell she was unusual, athletic, and damned good-looking. In fact, she was the most beautiful woman he'd ever seen, and he'd seen quite a few.

But you're not here to think about April, fella. You're here to get your life together. He gave the bathroom one more glance, squared his shoulders, and strode into the hall.

She'd set the table with plaid cloth napkins and place mats. A vase of roses he hadn't noticed this morning sat in the center, and two wineglasses glowed with amber light.

She turned when he entered the room. Something flared in her eyes, then it was gone. "I hope you like your steak medium-rare."

"That's exactly how I like it." His stomach rumbled at the smoky aroma. He sat down on the green ladder-back chair she indicated, then gazed at the plate she set before him. He noted the sprig of parsley tucked under the meat, a drizzle of butter over the asparagus, crumbled bleu cheese on the salad greens.

He took a swallow of the wine. Rich and mellow, with a hint of sweetness, and unlike any he'd tasted before. "What is it?"

"Dandelion." She settled in the opposite chair and gave a quick smile. "Last year we had a bumper crop."

"You make your own wine?"

"Sometimes. Depends on what's available. I've also got some elder blossom."

He stared at her. The ends of her hair curled around her shoulders like spun gold, and there was a healthy flush of pink on both cheeks. She met his gaze with large eyes, more gray than blue, fringed with light-brown lashes. She'd added some pink color to her lips, but even without it she was beautiful.

Her flannel shirt hid her figure, and for a wild instant, he wanted to see her without it, touch her silky flesh. He ached to bury his face in that gleaming hair.

His heart hammered so loudly he was sure she could hear it, but she gave no indication. He let out his breath and cut a bite of steak.

Forget it, McKittrick, you're not looking for a woman. He speared the piece of meat and stuffed it in his mouth. If he repeated that every time he looked at her, maybe he'd believe it.

After the meal she suggested coffee in the living room. They sat as they had the evening before, she in the red cushioned chair, he on the sofa. In the opposite corner he made out a tangle of paws where at least three cats curled into an indistinguishable mound of orange, black, and tabby fur. A lean dark-colored Siamese crouched on the scatter rug in front of the woodstove, and gave him a cross-eyed stare.

Tom couldn't think of a thing to say. She'd wanted to talk, so why didn't she say something?

The silence deepened. April looked cool and calm, a far cry from the mad lady in Wellingtons he'd seen earlier. Not a good sign, his instincts told him. He cleared his throat.

Tom took a long swallow of coffee and braced himself. "You wanted to talk?"

April stiffened in the chair. "I have something on my mind."

He smiled. "I know exactly what's on your mind. And

I have to compliment you on your approach. The bath was relaxing, the dinner excellent, but—"

"But what?" She let out an exasperated breath. "Mr. McKittrick, I need to impress upon you that I have a binding contract—a ten-year lease."

"You *had* a contract."

"The fact that your grandfather is dead does not alter my contract."

"What makes you think so?"

"Only if I default on the points of the agreement, namely, if I do not maintain the grounds or fail to pay my rent on time, does the contract become invalid."

She tented her fingers over one knee and focused on him. "I've kept my part of the agreement, now I'm asking you to keep yours."

He admired her spunk. He should just stop her right now, but it was fun watching her get steamed up. He stifled a yawn.

"You're not listening," she scolded. He heard the steel behind the smooth, even tone.

"Sorry. Go on." Damn, but that hot bath and the wine were making him sleepy. He dropped his gaze to his lap, struggled to keep his eyelids open.

"I said my staying here could benefit you."

"In what way?"

"Creggan grows prizewinning roses. The value of the property is increased because of it, and this would bring prestige and recognition to you. Plus, you have the roses themselves to enjoy all season long."

"I'd have that anyway, Mrs. Fairchild. Whether you're here or not."

"But you don't know anything about growing flowers!"

"I could learn." He sat forward, studying her face. "I see that the roses are important to you, but that's not enough, not for a woman like you. What's the real reason you want to stay?"

"I—" She dropped her head. "I have no place else to go. My herb business is here."

"And how is your business doing?"

She hesitated. "I manage to keep my customers satisfied."

He shook his head. "No, no. What's your ROI?"

She looked up, a puzzled expression on her face. "Uh, the lavender sachets sell well, but, um—"

"Return on investment, Mrs. Fairchild. How many clients? What's your marketing strategy?"

She looked away. "I sell every Tuesday at the farmers' market, and I have six retail customers in town."

He snorted, and set his coffee cup down on the end table. "It figures. Have you a current database? A Web site? Online ordering?"

"I don't have a computer." She gripped the arms of the chair, her tone defensive, and leveled her gaze with his. "I don't know about marketing methods as you do, but I know my product."

He noted her carefully modulated tone, observed the pride in her voice. "That, at least, is something."

The Siamese crept toward the sofa, fastened huge blue eyes on Tom, and leapt onto his lap. Tom shrank against the back cushion. "You need a marketing plan. But even without one, you can find another location and reinvest your savings. You have no overhead to speak of."

She turned toward the fire, her voice low. "I have little in savings. I can make ends meet, but if I can't harvest the flowers and herbs that are already established here at Creggan, then I have nothing to sell." She stretched her hand out in front of her, faced him again. Her eyes burned with a inner fire. "Look, Mr. McKittrick, I'm a good gardener, and I'm quiet. Let me stay. You'll never even know I'm here, except that your roses will be the pride of the entire valley."

He rose and looked her in the eye. "It's tempting, Mrs. Fairchild. Very tempting. But the answer is still no."

SIX

April stared at him for a long moment, then asked in a stiff voice, "If you weren't going to let me stay and run my business, why did you ask about my return on investment? As if you were really interested?"

The look in her eyes probed too deep for comfort. He *was* interested. In her. And he didn't want to be. He noted the reproach in her tone, and a band tightened around his chest. He tried to shake off the feeling of unease. "Be-cause—"

Oh, Jesus. He didn't want to explain, he just wanted to pull his life together. And he didn't need a distraction like April Fairchild around to complicate the process. He threw up his hands, spun on his heel, and stalked toward her workroom.

"Wait," she called after him. "I haven't finished!"

He froze at the threshold. Hell's bells, did she never give up? Gripping the doorknob, he drew in a huge breath. He'd feel the same way if he were in her shoes, but he needed time alone to think more than he needed prizewinning roses.

He ordered a calmness into his voice. "I'm sorry. There's nothing more to say. Good night, Mrs. Fairchild."

Tom tossed and turned. When sleep finally came, close to four A.M., he dreamed about April. She was loading her car with cages of cats, tears streaming down her cheeks. The accusation in her eyes made his gut clench.

When he awoke, he could still see her ravaged face, the wide, uncomprehending blue eyes. He glanced at the clock. Barely seven. He'd like to roll over and go back to sleep, but he had work to do. He rose, dressed hurriedly in charcoal trousers and an Italian knit sweater in shades of red and blue, and brushed his teeth.

The house was quiet, and April's bedroom door was closed. He moved toward the kitchen, then spotted her bent over, pouring kibble into cat dishes. She straightened, met his gaze, and turned away. The cat food rattled as it filled the bowls.

She was still mad. Fine. He could deal with that. He clamped his jaw shut and strode toward the front door. She made no move to stop him, which was just as well. Maybe if he didn't have to look into those soft, sky-colored eyes over the breakfast table, he'd feel less like a jerk.

The dewy grass squeaked under his soles. A robin sang from a trio of birches in the center of the meadow, and he slowed to listen. Odd, he'd never noticed how beautiful a birdsong could be. Not so odd, he amended. When had he taken the time to listen? Usually this time of morning found him in a weighty corporate meeting or dictating his daily schedule to his secretary.

But not anymore. He filled his nostrils with the clean scent of the surrounding pines, surprisingly glad he wasn't in a smoke-filled boardroom drinking coffee from a Styrofoam cup. Now, the question was, what the hell was he going to do here in Lupine Valley? Money wasn't a problem; he'd invested his stock options wisely. Winding down and reassessing his life were the sticking points.

He didn't have any answers. Hadn't figured it out yet. But when he got the bed and the chimney and the rest of the house sorted out, he'd at least have time to sit and think.

He picked up a leather work glove from the grass, examined it, then laid it on the woodpile. Too large for April. Must be Raven's. April had small, capable hands with close-trimmed nails. Working hands. He liked that.

In fact, he found himself liking a lot of things about his tenant. She seemed a little crazy at times, but she made sense in a way. No doubt about it, she'd improved his property, and she'd done it out of unselfish dedication.

A gray squirrel raced along branches, jumped from limb to limb along a line of tall fir trees. Man, what guts. A surge of admiration poured through him. If that little creature could conquer his world on guts and instinct, who was he to worry about a brief setback? He reached his front porch and took the steps two at a time.

At the maple breakfast table he wrote out a shopping list for himself and instructions for Raven, which he tacked to the front door, then charged down the steps to his car, turned the key in the ignition, and roared down the drive. He had a lot of things to do before the day was done.

By four o'clock when Tom pulled his Mercedes back onto the narrow lane that led to the estate, his shoulders ached and his feet felt as though he'd run the Boston Marathon. He'd hit every shopping mall he'd seen and walked at least five miles. Pacific Gas and Electric had promised his power would be turned on by noon, and the phone company said his new lines would be in by five. He hoped Raven had hauled the old bed off to the dump, but if the fellow had showed up on time it would surprise the hell out of him. At least with the power on, the house would be ready for the cleaning service and painters.

He steered his freshly washed car up the driveway, carefully avoiding the soft shoulder. Thoughts of hot water for a shave, and the new king-size bed he'd ordered, warmed him all the way to his toes.

Despite his sore muscles and the crowds, which he hated, it had been an upbeat day. He'd driven to Santa Rosa and bought all the kitchen and bath towels he could ever need, a set of fine German cutlery, cookware, and a barbecue grill. In the trunk were three pair of jeans, work boots, and a half-dozen soft flannel shirts. Finally, he laid in a week's supply of groceries. Tonight he'd celebrate with a juicy porterhouse and a bottle of Cabernet.

He slowed the automobile and stared across the meadow at his front yard. "What the hell?"

His new bed sat outside on the ground.

Tom jammed on the brake, switched off the ignition, and bounded up the porch steps. A note was nailed to the door frame. *Bed too big. Back tomorrow to remove door. Raven.*

"Too big?" Tom muttered. His new bed was going to sit out in the front yard until tomorrow?

He pivoted slowly and stared at April's cottage. Then he closed his eyes. He didn't even want to think about it.

Forcing his feet down the steps, he tramped to his car and opened the trunk. Loading four heavy grocery bags in his arms, he trudged into the house, dropped the bags on the breakfast table, and went back for the rest.

By the time he had everything unloaded, the sun hung low in the sky and long shadows stretched across the meadow. Jesus, he was tired. And hungry. The thought of a sizzling steak with mushrooms and a Roquefort salad made his mouth water. Duck soup, now that he had everything he needed. No need to bother April at all. He'd set up his barbecue and decant the wine. Then he'd put his feet up and think about camping out.

He strode into the kitchen and turned on the tap. A dribble of water trickled out of the faucet.

Tom groaned. What now? Were the pipes blocked? He tried again. This time the faucet sputtered and went dry. Oh, hell. He turned off the tap and scratched his head. Maybe he could ask April what was wrong.

He could, but he sure didn't want to. He'd stomped off to bed in a funk last night, and this morning she was icy quiet. He didn't want to ask her a damn thing.

But he had to have water. He squeezed his lids shut, counted to ten, and then marched out of the house and down the steps. There had to be a simple explanation.

As he walked, he searched the meadow for some kind of holding tank.

"Watch it!" a voice cried. A dirt-filled wheelbarrow careened to a stop, and he pulled up short. April released the handles and propped gloved hands on her hips. She wore a sky-blue tank top and form-fitting denim cutoffs. Her long, slim legs were tanned to a pale gold. His pulse charged into quick time.

She gave him a studied look. "Got your shopping done I see. Too bad about the bed."

Tom snorted. "Your friend sure didn't stick around for long."

She stiffened. "Raven has classes at night."

Tom arched an eyebrow. "Classes? What, in yoga?"

"He teaches physics at the community college," she answered in an even voice. She bent to pet a cat who sidled up and brushed against her bare leg.

"I—" He stepped around the wheelbarrow to face her. "I have a problem. There's no water."

April regarded him with curiosity. "Did you check the pump pressure control?"

Tom let out his breath in a hiss. "I don't know where the damned well is, much less the pressure control."

She laid her gloves on the wheelbarrow handle. "Wait here, I'll be right back." She marched across the meadow, and two minutes later returned with a canvas tote slung over one shoulder.

"C'mon." Without breaking her stride, she tramped toward the fir trees behind his house. Hidden among the trees stood a tall, green tank, and next to it sat a metal box on a post. April popped the cover off and peered inside.

"Here's your problem, a corroded wire." She cut the power to the box, clipped the wire at each connection, and then snipped a short length from a spool in her tote. In minutes she attached a new wire and switched on the power. The pump motor surged to life.

"That should solve the problem until next time."

"Next time?"

"It happens all the time. You get used to it living out here."

April watched Tom's face fall, and she nearly laughed out loud. Two lines furrowed his brow. "I see." He didn't look like he saw at all, but it was his problem, not hers. *Welcome to the country, Mr. City Mouse.*

She stuffed the spool of wire and her cutters in the tote, snapped the cover on the control box, and headed back the way she'd come.

Tom raced to catch up with her. "What other surprises am I in store for?"

She studied him while she strode along. "It's not something you can categorize. Sometimes a season goes by with nothing out of the ordinary. Other times problems develop every week."

"Name some."

"Well, in a wet or stormy winter, trees fall, creeks flood, the power goes out, sometimes for days. You'll need a chain saw and a generator. In the summer, the septic tank might need pumping. The well might go dry."

He didn't answer. Instead, he turned away and walked slowly toward his house. April watched the rhythm of his step, picked up her gloves, and pushed the wheelbarrow into the toolshed. The man was trying, she'd say that for him. She admitted she felt a twinge of sympathy every time he ran into a problem, but she was still so mad at him she resolved not to feel sorry for him. But between trying not to laugh at his predicaments and trying not to run him down with the wheelbarrow, she was exhausted. Fury and physical attraction, she thought with dismay, felt pretty much the same—a pounding heart and hot shivers up her spine.

Who needs it? She had problems enough. And a great big new one waiting just inside her front door this very minute.

April eyed the two large boxes beside her workroom door. She hoped to God she hadn't made a mistake. This morning she'd bought a computer. Tonight, after she completed the potpourri order for Mrs. Carson, she'd try to set up the equipment. The trouble was, she hadn't the foggiest idea where to start.

Tom McKittrick would probably find hooking it up easy; corporate executives were more at home with computers than well pumps. Tom's trouble, she mused, was he was too tied up in the big-city business world to know much about country life.

And, she realized with a jolt, *she* had been so tied up getting along in the country that she hadn't developed sufficient marketing skills to grow her business.

She stared at the computer boxes. Well, that was about to change.

When the knock rattled her front door, she knew right away who it was. She bit back a bubble of laughter. *What does Mr. City Executive need now?* Stepping around two cats, she reached the door and swung it open.

Tom stalked inside, a grocery bag in one arm, a bottle of wine in the other. He strode to the counter, plopped the bag down, and handed her the bottle.

"Dinner?" she asked, trying not to smile.

"Whatever it takes."

She cocked her head to one side and suppressed a rising elation. "That bad, huh?"

"Nothing is working out right. I've got lights everywhere but in the kitchen. No power. No explanation. I couldn't even find a breaker switch." He set his mouth in a grim line. "I feel like a fish out of water. I need help."

He pinned her with a frustrated look in his green-brown eyes. "I need your help."

A wild idea bloomed. So, Mr. Executive was crying uncle. It was too good to be true, but she wouldn't waste one minute analyzing it. He needed something from her, and now, for the first time, she had something concrete to bargain with.

"I just might be able to manage that," she said. "For a price."

He settled heavily into the ladderback kitchen chair. "Name it."

"Hook up my new computer."

For an instant his eyes widened. "Deal."

"Pour the wine?"

"You got it." He rose and took the bottle out of her hand. "Anything else?"

"You cook dinner."

"Sure, piece of cake."

"And let me stay in the cottage."

He studied her for a long moment. "I'll think about it—let you know after dinner."

Her heart did a queer little somersault in her chest. She'd come this far. She wouldn't—couldn't—think about any answer but yes.

She sipped her wine and suppressed a smile of triumph. "Dinner first. You get to unpack the computer."

"Oh, no. I'll cook. *You* unpack the computer. It will be educational."

She'd swear she saw a hint of laughter in his brown eyes and sent him a cool glance. "So will watching you cook dinner." In fact, she thought as she opened the first box, watching the city boy flounder in her kitchen ought to be downright entertaining.

SEVEN

Tom eyed the large, square boxes, then April. "Go on," he said, focusing on her face. "Watching you figure out where to plug in everything ought to be good."

April fortified herself with another sip of wine, then settled back against the sofa pillows. "After you, Mr. McKittrick. If your kitchen prowess matches your country-survival skills, dinner doesn't look promising." She refilled her glass, then folded her arms across her chest and waited for him to back out of their bargain.

It took him only two strides to reach the kitchen alcove. Shoving his sweater sleeves up strong, muscular arms, he pivoted to survey the countertop with its knife block, tiered vegetable basket, and spice rack. Bending at the waist, he peered inside her refrigerator.

Her gaze focused on his lean form as he sifted through the contents of the crisper. The cut of his trousers accentuated his long legs and trim backside. Definitely attractive.

Her breath hissed in. She'd never made a habit of studying men's backsides before. Not even ones as nice as Tom McKittrick's. It must be the wine.

He closed the refrigerator door, set salad greens, carrots, and a handful of mushrooms on the counter. Unable to tear her eyes away, she watched in disbelief as he tied her green striped apron around his waist and took two blue plates down from the shelf. He looked out of place and devilishly handsome. Opening drawer after drawer, he finally found the silverware, then laid two place settings, blue-and-green cloth napkins, and the plates on the table.

He turned toward her. "Charcoal?"

She jerked her gaze away from his eager, boyish expression. "In a pail beside the barbecue." Kneeling on the floor beside one of the boxes, she turned it right side up.

"Matches?"

"Over the stove." She sliced open the packaging tape on the smaller box. She'd bet he lacked Boy Scout skills as well. In a moment or two he'd be asking her to light the fire.

He grabbed the matches and strode out the rear door. Five minutes later he was back, but he didn't say a word. Instead, he sliced mushrooms, chopped a slice of onion into small bits. Setting them aside, he began to tear bite-size chunks of baby romaine into her polished-walnut salad bowl. She stared at his hands, at the long, straight fingers. As he worked, her attention moved to his arms. Muscles rippled in his forearms. Dark, curly hair dusted the smooth, pale skin.

With a shaking hand, April reached for her wineglass and gulped down a swallow. Watching the very masculine Tom McKittrick in her country kitchen made her uneasy. She tore her eyes away from him, plunked her glass

down, and concentrated on lifting the computer monitor
out of the box.

The pungent smell of mushrooms sautéing in butter
and garlic wafting into the living room made her stomach
rumble. She leaned forward to get a better look.

He jiggled the skillet of mushrooms over the gas
flame, then drizzled sherry from her grandmother's cut-
glass decanter over them. A cloud of fragrant steam rose,
and April licked her lips. She hadn't eaten since breakfast. And, unbelievably, everything smelled heavenly!

Using her favorite chef's knife, Tom sliced a scallion
with swift, sure strokes. Darned if he didn't look like he
knew exactly what he was doing! She'd never known a
man who liked to cook. Teddy had refused to make even
coffee.

Twenty minutes and another half glass of wine later,
April had the rest of the components unpacked and the
computer, keyboard, monitor, speakers, and program
disks arranged on her coffee table. She stared at the as-
semblage. She had absolutely no idea how to hook it all
together.

Tom strode in, a plate in one hand. "Ready?"

"So soon?"

He grinned and returned to the kitchen to set the platter of sliced steak in the middle of the table.

She scrambled to her feet, trotted after him, and lowered herself into the ladderback chair. Choking back an
exclamation, she stared at the food. Surrounding the
pink, juicy slices of meat were steamed carrots with parsley butter drizzled over them. In her blue vegetable dish,
the mushrooms mounded temptingly, glazed in their own

sherry sauce. A single fluted mushroom sat on top. Where had he learned to do that?

He grinned at her. In a flash she knew she looked like a goggle-eyed kid.

Careful not to glance up, she slid two chunks of steak onto her plate and spooned helpings of mushrooms and mixed green salad alongside. She was in no mood to acknowledge his triumph. If he so much as chuckled, she'd. . . .

She forked a bite of the steak with a mushroom slice and closed her eyes. Good. Better than good, it was divine! She'd fallen into her own trap. This man more than knew his way around a kitchen.

"You lied to me," she said over a mouthful of carrot.

He arched one dark brow, the grin fading only slightly. "I did not. I merely said I'd make dinner."

"But," she waved her fork at him, "you didn't tell me you could cook. I mean, not like this."

The corners of his mouth turned up. "I'd hardly volunteer if I couldn't. Besides," he said, his smile widening, "if I'd told you, I'd have missed your reaction. It was worth it just to see the look on your face."

"What look? What do you mean?"

"The one that's there now. The one that says you can't believe I didn't fall on my butt again." His eyes twinkled. "I may not be an expert wood stacker, but I can slice mushrooms and grill steak."

Heat flushed her cheeks. He certainly could. She wondered if he had other accomplishments as well. Nonculinary ones.

He hoisted the bottle, gestured toward her glass. "More wine?"

She shook her head. Her brain was already spinning. "I don't think I'd better."

He studied her, a curious expression in his green-brown eyes. Then pouring the remainder in his glass, he took a long swallow. "What made you decide to buy a computer all of a sudden?"

She started. "Something you said." She lowered her gaze. Watching his fingers curl around the glass, stroke the stem, ignited a flicker of awareness in her belly. She crossed her arms in front of her, trying to quash the feeling.

"I'd been thinking about it. When you mentioned on-line business, I realized it could help me gain customers."

"How much do you know about computers?"

She chewed on her lower lip. "Not much."

He frowned and let out a slow breath. "It figures." He wiped his mouth with his napkin. "You're too impulsive. Business people don't buy equipment simply because someone else suggests it would be a good idea. They do a market analysis, then decide."

April pushed her plate toward the center of the table and steepled her fingers. "I don't have time to analyze the market. I need more customers and I need them right now."

"Computers aren't for everyone. If you're willing to put in the time, you can make it work for you. But—"

"It *will* work. It has to work." She focused on the V-neck of his sweater where a thatch of dark hair gleamed against the backdrop of pale skin. She was finding it hard to keep her mind on computers. She rimmed her lower lip with her tongue.

"I'll make you a deal."

His eyes crinkled at the corners. "I thought we already had a deal. Dinner and setting up your computer in exchange for another night on the bed in your workshop."

"I've got a better one," she heard herself say. "My country know-how"—she gathered her courage and blurted the rest—"in exchange for letting me stay in the cottage."

He rose. His eyes had turned a rich peat moss brown, and they bored right through her. His jaw tightened. "Too one-sided. I never take on an investment where I don't have a better than fifty percent rate of return."

She leaped to her feet and faced him, jabbing her thumb against her chest. "You need me."

"I do, huh?" Both brows lowered. "Would you care to explain that?"

April gulped a breath. It was now or never; she'd better be convincing. "You know about computers and cooking—things you do in the city. But you don't know anything about wells or septic tanks or blocked pipes or . . . a thousand and one things out here in the country that I *do* know about."

He just looked at her.

"So it's plain as day, isn't it?" She tried to slow down her speech, but she was as wound up as a watch spring.

"What is?"

"It will save you money if you let me stay. I'll be your administrative assistant in the field, so to speak. Out here on your own, your dry-cleaning bills alone would probably amount to half my rent."

He leaned back against the table, cupping his chin in his palm. His eyes were shuttered, his forefinger extended up the side of his face, evaluating. Her throat tightened.

"So you see, Mr. McKittrick, it's to your advantage to let me stay. I can help you."

She reached for a dirty plate, but he stopped her.

"Leave it—I'll do the dishes. I need some time to think, and I do it better when my hands are busy." His mouth formed a hard, thin line. "Go sit by the fire. You can watch while I set up your computer."

Cobwebs had swathed her brain. She couldn't think of one intelligent thing to say. *So, okay, Mr. Thinking-It-Over, I'll curl up on the sofa and get my equilibrium back.* She plopped down among the soft pillows and watched him. A moment later he traipsed over and handed her a cup of hot tea.

She cradled the cup in both hands, took a sip, then rested her chin on her knuckles. This wasn't going a bit like she'd planned. She had to convince him that he needed *her,* not the other way around. "About our deal—"

Twin vertical lines etched his forehead. "You don't give up, do you?"

Maybe *he* did. But April Fairchild didn't. She took a deep breath. "You let me stay in the cottage, and I will teach you everything you need to know about living in the country." *Now, Mr. City Executive, try that for return on investment!*

His mouth tightening, he rolled his eyes toward the ceiling. For a split second he glanced away, then turned to her, his expression carefully neutral. "Where do you want the computer set up?"

"On the counter in my workroom. But if you could

set it up here, so I can watch, I'll take notes. Tomorrow I'll reassemble it in there."

"Seems like a lot of extra work, but . . . whatever." He shrugged and pulled a small silver screwdriver out of his pocket.

As he worked, she drank her tea and tried to focus on what he was doing, but her mind kept rehearsing her next argument about the cottage. A man like him wouldn't like being dependent on a woman. Maybe she should slant it more toward *her* needing *him?*

He hunkered down in front of the coffee table. "The connectors are all color-coded," he explained, pointing to the setup diagram. "This blue monitor cable fits into the blue connector right here on the back of the computer."

Tom hooked up the cable, then glanced at the woman who watched him. She had set her cup on the end table and flopped back against the pillows, a notepad propped on her knees. He had to hand it to her. She was one determined lady. He went back to the diagram, smiling inside at the scratch of her pencil on the paper.

An hour later, he had the computer set up and working. He ran through several systems tests, explaining in detail what he was doing to April on the sofa. Finally he switched the monitor off. "You're up and running."

April made no reply. Tom stood and peered down at her.

She lay curled in one corner of the sofa, her blond hair fanned out over the blue pillow, sound asleep. Well, well. So the lady dynamo who could stack wood and propel a loaded wheelbarrow about the place was human after all.

Something drew him closer, and he leaned forward for

a better look. In the lamplight, her skin looked like ivory satin.

A band coiled around his heart. Awake or asleep, April Fairchild was one intriguing—and beautiful—female. Part of him wanted to just stand there and look at her; another part wanted to get the hell out of the cottage.

He liked setting up the computer for her. Damn it, he liked *her*. But he didn't want to feel anything beyond that. He wanted to evaluate his professional life, decide what was important and what wasn't. For the first time since college, he felt the need to slow down and think about where he wanted to go from here, and he wasn't going to muddle it up with a woman.

Yeah, right, Tom. So why can't you make your feet move? He stood gazing at her until his neck began to ache.

Enough of this! He was tired. She was zonked out. *Hell, Mrs. Fairchild, let's get some sleep.* He gathered her up in his arms and wandered toward her bedroom.

She felt warm and soft in his arms, and she smelled of roses. A tiny pulse throbbed at the base of her throat. She made a sleepy, mumbling sound, and her head rolled against his chest. His heart hammered until he could barely breathe. He kicked her bedroom door open with his foot.

The room was so feminine he felt like tiptoeing. Lacy dresser scarves drooped over the mahogany highboy, and a quilted burgundy-and-ivory lace comforter covered the bed. A tan teddy bear in a red knitted vest sat in a maple rocker in the corner, a black cat snuggled against it. With one hand, he pulled the covers down, then lowered April onto the sheets. The instant he drew the comforter over her, a second cat hopped onto the bed and began to lick its fur.

He stared down at her face, noting the blush of rose over the high cheekbones, the slight bump on an otherwise straight nose. A fist slammed into his midsection. She looked so peaceful. Young and fresh and vulnerable. She might know how to grow prizewinning roses and make strawberry preserves, but she was a babe in the woods in the business world.

If he evicted her, she'd have to start over again. If he let her stay. . . .

He'd enjoy it. Like her more and more.

If he let her stay, he had trouble. Big Trouble.

Tom tossed on the narrow bed in April's workroom. He'd locked the door to keep the cats out, but still he couldn't sleep. April's face haunted him. Her warm, pliant body had felt so good in his arms, he hadn't wanted to let her go. Even now, he felt his groin stir.

Lord, he didn't *want* to want her. But standing by the bedside, watching the rise and fall of her breasts under the flannel shirt brought an economy-size load of uncontrollable feelings.

He flopped over onto his side. He admired April's spirit and, damn it, he wanted to help her. He had to smile at her offer—her cottage in exchange for country-living lessons. She needed him more than he needed her. He could teach her about marketing skills, help her get her product to a larger clientele. With a rush of exuberance, he realized he would be valued for his expertise, not his wealth. For the first time he could remember, something of his real self—not his position or his power—really mattered to someone.

He punched the pillow and settled his tense frame in a new position. April's indifference to either his money or his influence was refreshing. It also piqued his interest. When he thought about it, her indifference to him made him uneasy. Off balance. Women had always pursued him, made their interest in him blatantly clear. Which, he acknowledged, was flattering but flat somehow. They never asked what he thought about anything, the latest Oscar nominees, the struggles of wheat farmers in Iowa, not even the weather. All they wanted to know was when he would telephone them next.

He glanced at the alarm clock on the bedside table and sighed. The thought of April's need for his brain instead of his, well, body was intriguing. And disturbing. For one thing, she showed absolutely no interest in him physically.

And for another, she wasn't like any woman he'd ever known. Half of the time he didn't know what to make of her.

And to top it off, he was finding it hard to be around her without wanting to touch her.

April set the lid on the skillet to let the eggs cook, then buttered the toast. Nothing like a good breakfast to weaken a man's resolve. Even one as stubborn and unyielding as Tom McKittrick.

She glanced at him out of the corner of her eye when he strode into the room, and dropped the spatula on the countertop. A red-and-blue-plaid flannel shirt disappeared into rugged, snug-fitting denims. Her throat closed. Lordy, but didn't he look great in jeans! The slim cut showed off his rangy build to perfection.

Very nice. More than nice. She lowered her gaze. The loafers were gone, replaced by ankle-high work boots in a soft chestnut leather. Dragging her gaze back to the stove, she dished up the eggs and bacon, then poured a mug of coffee and set it at his place.

He glanced at the table but didn't move.

"Your breakfast's getting cold."

"Where's yours?"

"I'm not hungry."

Tom bit into the toast. "You try the computer yet?"

"Not yet. I . . . overslept. Actually, I didn't sleep too well."

"Damn right," he murmured.

Her cheeks burned. "I didn't finish taking notes, either."

"No problem."

"About our . . . our discussion last night—"

His mouth twitched. "Was that what it was? I thought it was a proposition."

April sucked in a quick breath. "Before you say anything, I have something to tell you. You see—" she took another breath to quiet the pounding of her heart—"I wasn't entirely honest with you last night."

His eyes darkened. "What do you mean?"

"It's true you need my knowledge of country ways, but more than that, I need something from you. I need you to teach me how to manage my business."

There. She'd said it. She'd played her trump card. It was the oldest female ploy in the books, but she prayed

Mr. Invincible had a perfectly normal male soft spot. She cupped her hands around the mug, watched his expression, and waited.

He eyed her with an odd light in his eyes, but seemed in no hurry to answer. He forked a bite of egg past his lips, and chewed thoughtfully.

The silence lengthened.

Hell's bells. If he was going to say no, why didn't he just say it and get it over with.

Finally, she couldn't stand it any longer.

She scraped her chair back and stood. "I have things to do."

His dark eyebrows rose. "You aren't going to wait for my answer?"

She stared at him. "Your silence is answer enough."

"Mrs. Fairchild, I made up my mind last night. I should have told you right away, but I kinda wanted to hear what you'd come up with next." A smile tugged at the corner of his mouth. "You know, you're the most maddening woman I've ever met."

"Maddening? Me? I think I've behaved very well considering the situation."

He chewed on a mouthful of bacon. "Okay. Maybe maddening is too strong. How about obstinate?"

Her blood pressure rose until she thought her brain would explode. Maddening? Obstinate? Who was he to complain?

She snatched her mug off the table and started for the kitchen counter. "Well, now you've heard what I've come up with, so tell me!"

"Are you always this hot under the collar?" His smile angered her even more than his words.

"Yes! No! Just *tell* me. I can't stand waiting to see if my world is going to come crashing down around me."

"I see. Wouldn't you—"

"No, I wouldn't. Just get it over with."

He caught her wrist and pulled her back into her seat. "Okay. Okay." He stared down at her, one hand still gripping her wrist.

"Well?" Near tears, April fought to keep her frustration from showing.

"Well," he said in a low, purposeful voice, "what I wanted to tell you is I've decided to . . ."

April yanked her hand into her lap and lowered her head. She knew the answer. He wouldn't go for it. "You're making a big mistake, you know."

"Oh, I know," he said with a grin. "Probably a real doozy, too."

"Absolutely."

"You can stay."

"I'll start pack— What?"

"I've decided to accept your deal."

April stood up. "You have?"

"But," he continued, "there is one small condition."

EIGHT

April's breath caught. Had she heard him right? Tom was actually going to let her stay at the cottage? Elation surged through her. But wait a minute! He'd said something else. . . .

Her euphoria fizzled like a rain-soaked match. She stared at him, her eyes narrowing. "What condition?"

"Don't treat this as anything more than an expedient *temporary* business agreement. Each of us has something the other needs." He finished his bacon, took a swallow of coffee, and stood.

"Do you know your cheeks get red when you're mad?" He spoke in the same matter-of-fact tone he'd use to ask the time of day.

She bristled. "Stick to the subject, McKittrick. And they certainly do not." She snatched the plate from him, plunked it on the counter, and faced him. "I have conditions, too."

His mouth twitched. "And they are . . . ?"

"Don't block my driveway, and don't sweep out the eggs hatching in your chimney."

A warm light flashed in his eyes. "Wouldn't dream of it."

"Don't tell me how to run my life, and. . . ." She hesitated.

"And . . . ?" he prompted, his eyes murky as the hidden pond. Butterfly wings fluttered inside her stomach.

"You give me complete control of the garden."

He raked his fingers through his hair. "For a minute you had me worried. Believe me, Mrs. Fairchild, I wouldn't dream of interfering in your gardening. All I ask is that you teach me about country survival."

"On condition that you teach me how to grow my business."

"Fair enough." Tom leaned back against the counter, studying her face. She glanced at his plaid flannel shirt, the top button left undone, noticed how it fit across his broad shoulders, then gazed at his firm jaw and straight nose.

He had the most incredible eyes, she decided. Not brown and not green. He was a mix himself—part big-city executive, part loner. It had been a long time since she'd been around a man as complex as Tom McKittrick. She'd vowed to forget about men, but this one interested her. In a way she felt an odd sense of camaraderie with him. If they could share the estate and work in peaceable proximity, they might even enjoy being neighbors.

She planted her hands on her hips. "And one more thing."

He froze. "One . . . more thing?"

Her gaze lingered on his expanse of chest. *No more sexy sweaters.*

Good Lord, where did that thought come from? She

straightened her shoulders. "You come over only when I invite you."

The muscles in Tom's neck corded. "What the hell kind of condition is that?"

April studied a worn spot on the beige linoleum. "When I work on certain projects I . . . uh . . . can't be interrupted and. . . ." She looked up, focusing on the wall behind him. It was a lame excuse, but the only one she could think of at the moment. The truth was, he was a very sexy man, and . . . well, she didn't want to be distracted.

"I see," he said in a quiet tone. His accusing eyes suggested he didn't see at all, and she stiffened.

"I'm to help you straighten out your business, get your marketing quota up, but only when you aren't too busy, is that it?" He shoved his hands into his pockets, stepped into a wide-legged stance. "Sounds pretty at your beck and call to me."

Her heart gave a little thunk. "Oh, I only meant—"

His features softened the merest fraction. "I know what you meant, Mrs. Fairchild. Don't worry, I won't disrupt your schedule. I'll have a rather full one myself." He started for the door. "Okay, when you require my services, just leave a note on my door or"—he scribbled something on a scrap of paper—"telephone me. I'll leave my answering machine on."

Head down, Tom strode purposefully back toward his house. Did April Fairchild have a problem with men in general or just him? Every time she opened her mouth, another restriction came out. *Come when I call. Don't interrupt me.* Sounded like she didn't want anything to do with him, and boy, did that punch his buttons! Okay Miss Don't-Call-Me-I'll-Call-You, he'd leave her to sort it out. He had work to do.

He stumped up the front porch just as Raven's battered pickup bumped up the lane and skidded to a halt ten feet from him. "Yo, Tom. Ready to lug that monster bed inside?"

Tom squinted into the truck's cab. A brown leather vest flapped open over a mass of ginger-colored chest hair that matched his ponytail. Round turquoise beads, strung on a length of rawhide, nestled in the curly pelt.

Tom's mouth thinned. "Yeah, I am. Let's get a move on." The command came out gruffer than he had planned.

Raven cocked an eyebrow. "Kinda testy, huh, man? We got all day."

"Sorry." He flicked his gaze back to April's cottage. "It's been an interesting morning."

"April throw you a curve? Hey, man, don't pay her any mind. She's good people, just gets a burr under her saddle every now and then." He eased the truck forward. "Let's get that door off."

The pickup lunged ahead, then halted in front of the house with a squeal of brakes. Raven leaped out, a carpenter's apron clutched in one hand.

Tom surveyed the younger man's tie-dyed drawstring pants and sandals. He was either very competent or very foolhardy. Tom wiggled his toes inside his sturdy work boots.

It took Raven ten minutes to remove the door and another thirty to cut away the molding. Finally, the two of them jockeyed the massive headboard across the threshold. When the pieces lay in the bedroom, Raven began assembling the frame.

When Tom stepped into the living room to get the mattress slats, he heard footsteps on the porch. April stood in the open doorway, her hands curled around a green mug.

She gave him a tentative smile. "There's no door, so I just came on in. Where's Raven?"

"In the bedroom." She spun toward the hall and disappeared.

Well, I'll be damned. She'd brought only one cup, and it wasn't for him. He grabbed the slats and followed.

"Hey, babe," Raven called. Latching onto the mug with one hand, he enveloped her in a bear hug with his free arm.

Tom's pulse surged. *Keep your hands off her, you big oaf!* He bit back the remark and cleared his throat instead.

Raven disengaged his arm, shot Tom a curious look, then raised the mug to his lips. "Peppermint spice. Thanks, babe. You saved my life."

Tom gritted his teeth. Babe? Did those two have something going? Did April insist on appointments with Raven, as she did with him?

None of your business, mister. He shoved the thought aside and concentrated on setting the bed slats at equal intervals along the frame. Then he eyed the box spring. "Raven, want to give me a hand with this?" He hoisted one end of the bulky frame.

The younger man handed April his mug and grabbed the other end. Together they set the damask-covered box spring on the oak bed frame, then maneuvered the quilted mattress on top.

"Man, oh, man." Raven whistled. "That's some fine workbench."

April sucked in an audible breath, and Tom barely clamped a lid on his chortle.

Raven grinned. "You want it right here?"

"Right there is fine." He rubbed his chin with one forefinger. "Maybe center it more."

April backed toward the doorway and gave the bed a critical once-over. "May I make a suggestion?"

"Uh-oh," Raven murmured. "That's my cue. Gonna go wrestle that door." He gave Tom a gap-toothed grin as he clumped off.

Tom glanced at April. "You have a suggestion? Shoot."

She pivoted toward him and pointed to the adjacent wall. "I think you should put the bed there."

Tom shrugged. "Why? Will that help me sleep better?"

"It'll help you get up better."

Her comment made no sense. "One wall's the same as the other, except there's more room on this one."

"That's not the important point."

He rolled his eyes. "I give up. What is the important point?"

She trotted over to the bed. "You're in bed. You raise your head and what do you see?"

Tom thought a moment. "My dresser and the closet door."

"Exactly. Not inspiring."

"Does it have to be?"

She marched over to the other wall and faced him. "Imagine the headboard's here. Now, what do you see?"

He blinked. What kind of game was she playing?

"Come on, stand over here and then look," she commanded.

He sucked in a quick breath. What was with her? "Boy, are you bossy. Twenty minutes ago I said you could stay in the cottage and already you're ordering me around."

She chewed on her lip, then drew her mouth into a compressed line. "Just come over and stand here. You'll see in a minute."

He closed the space between them and followed her gaze.

Twenty yards beyond the window the hedge of red-and-white roses opened onto a secluded water garden. Rocks surrounded a kidney-shaped pond with a garden bench overlooking it. An arched bridge crossed the water, and a pair of white geese floated beneath it.

"Where did *that* come from?"

A smile flashed. "I built it. It was your grandfather's secret meditation spot. You can see it only from this window." She faced him with an "I told you so" look. "It's good feng shui. Against that wall"—she pointed to where the bed stood—"bad feng shui." She looked like a cat with its fur fluffed.

"If you say so." He didn't have a clue what she was talking about, and he wasn't sure he wanted to know. But, he acknowledged, that hidden garden, now that was another story. "Is this part of my country-living course?" he asked.

"I thought you'd want to see it before you decided where to place the bed."

"Yeah, you're right. Got any other ideas? I'm about to start painting."

"What color paint?"

"White. All my apartments have been white."

She frowned. "It figures. I'd expect a CEO to pick white. Or maybe the CEO's interior decorator picked it."

"You've got some really strong opinions. What's wrong with white?"

She shrugged. "Nothing, really. It blends with everything, but it's . . . well, it's kind of insipid."

"Insipid," he echoed.

She wrinkled her brow. "Sorry. I guess I do have strong opinions, but I've always thought of myself as an artist. I've got a good eye, and—"

"Yeah, you get an A for having a good eye, but you're flunking salesmanship."

Her eyes widened. "Oh, but I really do have good ideas, I—" She stared at him. "At least people usually tell me they're good."

He leaned his weight on one hip and crossed his arms. He'd swear he detected the slightest quaver in her voice. Maybe her confidence was just bravado. Maybe underneath she was a bit uncertain. "Okay, convince me."

"Well, for starters, I—" She spread her hands, palms up. "I wouldn't paint anything just plain white."

"You wouldn't." Tom kept his voice even, but his temper threatened to flare. He wasn't used to having his ideas challenged.

"Definitely not. I'd . . . let's see." She danced across the floor, peered at the window, then the wall. "With the morning light coming in"—she pivoted toward the bed, skimmed the smooth headboard with her fingers and swung around to face him—"I'd use buff stippling over a soft ivory with a touch of peach and green."

"Stippling? What's stippling?"

"You daub on paint with a sponge." She cupped her hand around an imaginary sponge and made little bouncing motions on the wall.

"Not in *my* bedroom you don't," he said in a tone that was gruffer than he'd intended. "No sponges. No stippling."

April looked crestfallen. "I think it would look beautiful."

"I don't want it beautiful. I want it plain. Restful. Why are we arguing about this, anyway?"

"Because you're a . . . man." She thrust her chin out. "How many apartments have you painted?"

He ground his teeth together. "None, but why should that matter?"

"Because you have no expertise here, and I do, and you're not willing to listen."

"So?"

"So, you're being pigheaded. I think you're afraid to try something different."

"*I'm* pigheaded? You barge in here with tea for . . . everybody but me and tell me how to arrange my furniture and paint my walls and then you say *I'm* pigheaded?"

"Well, maybe you're just stubborn."

"And you are . . . ?"

"Artistic. I see things, things that would look wonderful, and sometimes I can't keep my mouth shut."

Suddenly she looked like a kid caught with her hand in the cookie jar, and a stab of sympathy jolted through him. "Maybe we have different tastes."

"Or different values." She flung the words at him.

"Let's say different backgrounds. I've lived in the city all my life. You haven't."

Her cheeks turned pink. "Let's get back to pigheaded. I think for all your city living, you're really resistant to change, even something as simple as a different color for your walls. I call that pigheaded."

"I call it conservative."

She crossed her arms over her waist. "Whatever. Just because you've retired to the country doesn't mean you have to do things the same old way you always have. Why not be creative? Try new things." She waltzed to the center of the room, then spun toward him and halted just five feet in front of him. "What are you afraid of?"

Tom drew in a deep breath. She didn't realize how close she'd come to hitting the mark. It made him uneasy all of a sudden. He spoke without thinking, something he never did.

"You're the one holed up here in the woods like a hermit. What are *you* afraid of?" He strode to the window and turned away from her. "What are you running away from?"

A shadow passed over her face. "I'm not running away. I'm living a sane, quiet life on my own. I made that decision after Teddy died."

He pinned her with a direct gaze. "I don't buy that. You're rationalizing, afraid of the real world. That's why your flower business bottomed out."

She wrinkled her brow. "It has *not* bottomed out. It's just, uh, a bit flat right now."

"Want to bet? One look at your account books will confirm it. You're going under, aren't you?

"No! Well, maybe a little bit."

"I'll go over your business records tonight."

"Good," she snapped, stepping back to the wall. "I'll start stippling your bedroom walls."

"No, you won't," he said quietly.

"Hey, you two." Raven poked his head in the door. "You have all week to bicker. Me, I got other jobs waiting."

April's eyes glinted like pale-blue crystals. "We aren't bickering. We're, uh, negotiating." She stalked over to the window.

Raven chuckled, and Tom caught the younger man's eye. "You remounted the door?"

Raven nodded. "Better'n new. Hey, you two, go to it. I'm outta here."

Tom tossed Raven a nod, then turned back to April. "Where were we?"

April straightened and thrust both hands on her hips. "You're trying to intimidate me with your business talk. You—"

"We were discussing you, not me," Tom shot back. Her stance reminded him of a bantam rooster, feathers fluffed and ready for battle. His heart flip-flopped. He threw up his hands. "Okay, enough! You don't stipple and I won't check your books until you say so. Agreed?"

She stared at him a long minute, then stuck out her arm. "Agreed."

He enveloped her hand in his. It was warm and soft,

and trembled slightly. Reaching out with his other hand, he sandwiched hers between his own.

She snatched her fingers away and turned to go. "McCarty's in Santa Rosa has lots of . . . white paint."

Laughter bubbled up from his throat. She was exasperating. But mad as she was, she looked as cute as hell. He bit back a smile. He was beginning to enjoy this.

"Leaving so soon?" he heard himself say. "If you stay, we could discuss hanging curtains or even new carpeting."

"I'm going home," she said in a tight voice.

"What for? Have you run out of fang shoe?"

"Shway. Feng shway. I'm going"—she frowned—"to use the phone. I'll leave a message for you on your answering machine." She started toward the door.

"Before you go," Tom called, "want to help me move this bed over to the fang shoe—shway—wall?"

April spun around, her eyes wide. "You *want* to move it over there?"

Tom grunted. "Wouldn't want bad fangs or shoes," he joked.

A smile hovered on her lips. She marched to the opposite side of the bed and yanked up on the frame. She teetered unsteadily but managed to hoist the end up. She didn't look big enough to move a wheelbarrow, let alone an oak bed frame.

"Forget it. It's too heavy for you. I'll get Raven to help me in the morning."

She muttered something under her breath. "Don't make assumptions!" She eased the bed down, her eyes flashing. "I'm stronger than I look. Let's move it now."

"You'll hurt yourself."

"I won't either," she snapped.

Tom felt his hackles rise and just managed to keep a lid on his temper. "All right, then. You say when it gets too heavy." He heaved his side up and staggered under the weight. How in the world could she do this? He set his end down and strode to her side. "We'll shove it over instead."

April coaxed her end, inch by inch. When they reached the right spot, he straightened. His arms ached.

"No, it's not quite right. Over there, a little."

He groaned and shoved it six inches farther.

"Right there," she said. She darted to the window, stopped, and eyed the bed. "It's exactly right," she pronounced.

"Thank God for that," Tom breathed. "Next time I need something really heavy moved, I'll ask you."

The corners of her mouth turned up and for a minute he thought she was going to smile. She didn't. She hesitated for a split second. "Telephone first." Then she pivoted toward the door and marched out.

"Well, I'll be damned," he murmured. "So the herb lady has a sense of humor." He gazed out the window from the bed. April was right, the view was definitely better over here. Her theory was mumbo jumbo to him, but she had good ideas. She had other nice assets too come to think of it. He tried not to think about her blue-gray eyes and sunlit hair and the bewitching curve of her mouth. No good. The image of her shoving his bed, her cheeks puffed out with the effort, stayed with him.

He stared out at the little private garden. Tomorrow morning he'd stroll out there and sit on that bench. Maybe see about getting some koi for the pond.

He pulled two down pillows and a white comforter from the packing box, then dug in the bottom for the set of white sheets. He made up the bed, then lowered himself onto one corner and stretched out against the headboard. He gazed up at the wall. Yeah, white was practical, but maybe she was right. Maybe he was ready for something more exciting.

Stippling, she called it. Blotting with a sponge. Sounded crazy, but he'd felt so tied in knots for the last week a little craziness might be just what he needed. Lord knows, he'd had plain and regulated, and all of a sudden he was tired of it.

A picture flashed in his mind. He was fourteen, poised on the ten-meter diving board at the high school gym. He remembered wondering what he was doing up there; he didn't know the first thing about diving. He'd jumped into the pool holding his nose for the past eleven years, but that day, for some reason, it wasn't enough. Been there, done that. Besides, Jenny Feldman was watching.

Tom chuckled at the memory. He must have been nuts. He'd brought his arms up over his head, closed his eyes, and tipped forward off the board. He'd thought for sure he was going to die when he hit the water, but he didn't.

And now, forty miles away from the nearest swimming pool, he felt exactly the same way.

Tom brought his arms up over his head, pointed his fingers up, and closed his eyes. Yeah, he might try it again.

NINE

April tied the last rose petal and lavender sachet bag with a length of bright-pink ribbon, looping the ends into a floppy bow. The bags, all one hundred six of them, had taken her two days to stitch, stuff, and tie. Now, as she looked over the cardboard box brimming with pink-and-purple-printed cotton sachets, each sporting a pink APRIL'S GARDEN label, her backache eased. And her anxiety increased.

She should have arranged for her first business-management lesson with Mr. Executive Marketer, but getting her product ready for the Tuesday market had seemed more important. The sachets were ready. Now she'd run out of excuses to avoid him.

Face it, girl, any reason to stay away from Tom McKittrick is important. His broad shoulders and tight-fitting Levi's reminded her she'd been alone for six years. But trying to teach herself the accounting program Tom installed on her new computer had ended in futility. No matter what she did, she couldn't get it to work, and finally she'd switched off the bright, blue computer screen and that damned blinking cursor.

Tom could, a small voice murmured. She shook the thought aside and fastened her gaze on an orange-throated grosbeak perched in the damson plum tree outside her workroom window. Yes, Tom could do it. So, why didn't she just call him?

Because you're afraid of him, kiddo. Tom reminded her of things she didn't want to think about. Sometimes, late at night, she recalled the few good times before Teddy started treating her as one of his collectibles.

April swallowed, pushing down the bitter taste that rose in her throat. Teddy collected things: cars, expensive gadgets. Women. She had simply been part of his acquisitions, a well-dressed accessory when he traveled the racing circuit. When he grew restless, he simply added some other pretty woman to his retinue.

But she'd cared about Teddy, and it had been painful to feel left out. Discarded as if she were not important. After Teddy's death her family expected her to move back to Fallbrook. Instead, she did the unthinkable. She left New England and everything that reminded her of her husband and hadn't looked back.

Love hurt too much, she'd decided. She vowed never to care about a man again.

Sunlight caught the faceted prism in the window, sending a shower of color onto the opposite wall. She studied the spectrum. All the colors of the rainbow, displayed in the same reliable pattern. An immutable law of nature, like the cycle of the seasons. In some ways, like her work cycle on the estate. She clung to it because it gave her a sense of predictability.

She had Tom McKittrick to thank for letting her continue to stay in the cottage, use the flowers and herbs in the gardens for her livelihood. But her survival depended on her business skill, and she needed help. She needed *him*. She couldn't put it off any longer.

She marched into the kitchen and dialed his number. She got his answering machine. "I'm ready for Business 101 now." She drummed her nails on the counter. Answering machines were so annoying. He might call back. He might also be busy all day and not get the message until tonight.

Shadow strolled past, brushing against her legs. He raised one paw and scratched at the front door. "You want out, don't you, boy? Well, so do I." She retied one blue sneaker, straightened, then marched to the door. "Let's go see what the lion's doing in his den."

She headed across the meadow, then gave herself a brief mental once-over. She'd lived alone out here for so long she never gave a thought to how she dressed; the faded cutoffs and scoop-neck blue knit top were the first garments her gaze fell on this morning. All at once she realized how much of her skin showed. She gave the shorts a tug and hiked up the neck of the top.

Men's voices filtered through the trees. She glanced up to see a white van parked beside Tom's silver Mercedes, FAHY PAINTING splashed across the side in bright-red letters. She imagined men in white coveralls rolling all Tom's walls in endless expanses of Executive White.

Just as she started up the front steps, Tom burst through the doorway, his attention buried in a book. He had on tight-fitting jeans and a black T-shirt that accentuated his muscular arms. She forced her attention to the book's cover. *Painting Techniques Simplified*. He wheeled to the right without looking up.

"Did you get my message?"

He jerked his attention from the page, a touch of annoyance in his green-brown eyes. "What message?" He stared at her face, then moved his gaze lower. She felt his scrutiny of her chest all the way down to her toes. Next time she'd wear her flannel shirt.

"On your answering machine."

His face clouded. "I haven't had time for messages. I've got a crisis here. I was just coming to see you."

Her mouth curved. "Your drain's clogged?"

"The painters are having trouble."

She let out a quick breath. Since when did painters have trouble painting?

He motioned her inside.

Two coverall-clad men argued in one corner of Tom's bedroom. They hushed when April stepped in. The older man, apparently the one in charge, eyed Tom, an anxious look on his mahogany features.

"We no do zis before."

Tom muttered something and turned to April. "They don't understand stippling."

He'd changed his mind! Warmth coiled around her heart. He'd listened to her!

April circled the room. The walls wore a fresh coat of flat ivory paint. On the floor she spied cans of buff, peach, and green paint, an aluminum tray, and a large brownish-colored natural sponge.

Tom waved the book at her. "There's nothing in here that explains how much paint to stipple with."

She reached for the book and peered at the open page. "Stippling simplified." She gazed at Tom and felt a stab

of sympathy in her midsection. He looked totally flummoxed.

"It's a learned technique. Trial and error." He was really going to do it! Suddenly she wanted to dance around
the room.

One of the painters stepped forward, waggling his
brush. "We paint walls with brush, roller. No use
sponge."

"Just great," Tom muttered.

April held her smile in check. "I'll do the stippling."
She gave Tom a pointed look. "On one condition."

Tom rolled his eyes. "I'm not sure I want to hear any
more 'conditions.' "

"Show me how to set up a database." She waved her
arm at the painters. "Tell them to go home. Tell them
you've hired me instead."

Tom snapped the book closed. Then he turned to the
workmen. "You heard the lady. She's the stippling expert."

The painters mumbled something and began gathering
up their equipment. "Leave the ladder," Tom said, pulling
out his billfold. "I'll pay you for it."

When the men shuffled out, Tom turned to April. "I
hope to God you meant that. You have no idea how hard
it was to get any painting help up here. How long will
it take to finish?"

"I'll be done by dinner. Each coat dries fast." She bent
over the paint cans, poured a pool of the buff color into
the tray, and grabbed the sponge.

"You're starting already?"

"The sooner I finish, the sooner I get my database
lesson." She dragged the ladder over to one corner, set

the tray on the ladder shelf, and mounted the first rung. The ladder wobbled, and she thrust her hand against the wall to steady herself.

"Watch yourself," Tom cautioned.

"I will." She dipped the sponge in paint, daubed the excess on the tray, then reached into the corner and applied the paint with quick, light pats. Tom hovered behind her, watching.

"That looks wild."

"Wait until you see the green and peach added to it."

"Where'd you learn to do this?"

"From a book, just like you." She dipped the sponge into the last of the paint, patted it on the tray. "I like to experiment."

She stretched to reach an area near the ceiling, and without warning, the ladder tipped. April felt herself plunge sideways. She scrabbled for something to hold onto and felt the hard shoulder of Tom McKittrick.

He lunged for her. "Watch out."

She twisted sideways, her foot tangled in the rungs. A split second later, she found herself hauled firmly into Tom's arms, her breasts pushed against his chest. The empty paint tray clattered onto the floor.

"You all right?" Tom asked. His hands burned against her skin.

Her head swam, her mouth felt like the Sahara. A golf ball-size lump formed in her throat. "I'm not sure." Unable to take her eyes off him, she shivered.

He held her a moment more, his eyes boring into hers with a curious, startled expression. Then he dipped his head toward her.

He was going to kiss her! It was happening so fast

she couldn't think. His breath whispered over her skin. She watched his mouth descend and stood still, unable to move.

He smelled of musk and spice. When his lips touched hers, a current jolted through her. His mouth was warm and soft and demanding. A fire kindled deep in her belly.

The kiss went on for what seemed like minutes, until her thoughts tumbled like a stream over smooth stones. His mouth awakened a wave of longing, and she began to tremble. Tightening his grip on her arms, he deepened the kiss.

Her head spun. She didn't want this. At least the sensible part of her didn't. Suddenly, she tore herself free.

She eased out of his grasp and stepped away on rubbery legs. Forcing a steadiness into her limbs, she faced him.

He looked dazed and seemed to have trouble breathing. She watched his chest heave.

"Why did you . . . ?"

Lines of concentration deepened along his brows. "I'm not sure."

"I've always thought a man who kisses a woman knows what he's doing."

"I knew what I was doing." His low, rich cognac tone sent a quiver up her back.

She scrambled for something to say. "Familiarity complicates and we agreed to— This isn't part of our bargain."

He fisted both hands, then let them drop. "Damn it, April. Why do you have to dissect everything? Does there have to be a reason? Can't I kiss you just because I want to?"

He kissed her because he wanted to? Her heart tumbled, and then a band tightened around her chest. She focused on him for a long moment, crossed her arms, and looked pointedly away. "No, you cannot."

He made a quarter turn and faced her, a distinct hardening in his eyes. "Jesus, April, you don't make it easy for a man."

"I didn't invite you to kiss me."

He lifted one brow, his eyes glinting. "Seems to me like you enjoyed it."

"Well, I didn't," she snapped.

But she had enjoyed it. Too much. That was the problem. She liked her life here, liked her independence and being alone. She wanted it to continue.

She bent to retrieve the paint tray. Thank God it had been empty. She poured in a small pool of buff paint, retrieved the sponge, and set to work once more on the wall. Thoughts whirled in her head like leaves in the wind, and her hand shook. She forced herself to take slow, steady breaths.

Tom stepped in front of her, studying her with grim intensity. "That'll keep."

She pushed by him and started on a broad area by the window. "I'd just as soon finish today."

"You don't have to finish today."

"Yes, I do. We made a bargain. I need my lesson."

Tom frowned. "I think you're deceiving yourself," he remarked without inflection.

Seething inside, she daubed paint on another wall. Kidding herself, was she? What gave him the right to pronounce judgment on her? For that matter, what gave him the right to kiss her?

She turned her back on him and ran her fingers over her mouth. Her skin still tingled where his lips had touched. He tasted of coffee and mint, and he smelled clean, like a sun-drenched meadow. She'd liked being kissed. By him.

She slapped the sponge against the wall, smearing the paint. Damn. She snatched a damp cloth from the floor and rubbed out her mistake.

Tom strode into his kitchen, strangely lightheaded. Kissing April Fairchild had been the last thing on his mind this morning, but now that he'd done it, he knew he'd wanted to since the day he laid eyes on her. Beautiful, opinionated, and just a little bit cat crazy, his herb-growing tenant had tumbled his world in less than a week. He hadn't expected to find her attractive or even like her, but he did, and he wanted to touch her again, wanted to feel her lips on his. And, he thought, his blood racing, he wanted her legs wrapped around him.

Wait a minute. April was a distraction he didn't need right now. His brain still reeled from that kiss, but it wasn't the right time to get involved. He needed time to sort out his life, not a relationship.

He had to get out of the house.

The water garden was even more beautiful up close. As he passed under a latticed rose arch, a vista opened up that he hadn't noticed from the window. Blue-violet irises clustered near the water's edge, and beyond that he glimpsed the fresh green of the meadow and taller clumps of some other grasses with striped leaves. Flat rocks edged the pond, and lily pads dotted its surface.

He peered into the dark water. It must have required a lot of work to dig the pond and haul all that rock. April probably had help. His jaw suddenly tensed. Raven.

Tom let out his breath in a noisy hiss. He had to stop thinking about April and her admirers. He had no claim on her. He was reacting like an adolescent.

A bubble broke the still water and formed widening rings as an orange shape darted near the surface. Tom knelt on a rock and scanned the depths. Yes, there were fish in the pond. A pale one, two black ones, and a solid orange. A family, maybe.

He got to his feet and strolled to the bench. From here he could watch the fish and listen to the birds. And think about his life.

April had created this spot for herself, and now he'd come. He gazed over the water to the hedge of red and white roses. He provided the cottage and she cared for the grounds. He could live with that. Relish it, even. He didn't want a relationship, but, damn, he wanted April.

But that didn't stop him from remembering the feel of her firm body or the swell of her breasts against his chest, or the scent of lavender in her hair. And it did nothing to diminish the hunger he'd felt when he'd tasted her lips.

The sun moved low on the horizon, the golden light flickering dimly through the dark fir trees. Tom roused himself and glanced at his watch. Good Lord, he'd dreamed away the afternoon!

He shook his head and chuckled. It felt good not to worry about time. It felt so good that he was going to come back tomorrow and do it again. But now, he had a database lesson to get through.

He stood and started for the house. Should he offer her some dinner? No, he'd go over to the cottage later, give her the lesson, and get the hell out of there. He picked up his pace as he strode through the grass. Some things weren't meant to be.

By the time he reached his back door, he realized that as much as he wanted to avoid getting involved with April, he did look forward to seeing her. He'd be careful. She'd made it plenty clear that this was a business arrangement.

TEN

April rinsed the sponge and paint tray, set them on the kitchen counter, and wandered back into the bedroom to survey her handiwork in the fading light. She rotated her stiff neck while studying the stippled walls and let out a sigh of satisfaction. The green and peach paint added rich overtones to the pale buff, creating a marbleized effect. "See if that doesn't float your boat, Tom McKittrick," she challenged the empty room.

She raised her arms to the ceiling to stretch out the kinks in her back muscles, then on impulse flopped onto Tom's big bed and lowered her torso onto the canvas drop cloth covering the mattress. Feather softness cushioned her body, not too firm, not too spongy. Closing her eyes, she turned her cheek to the pillow. A hint of his spicy aftershave wafted up through the coarse cloth.

Her breath hitched, and she bolted upright. Lying on Tom McKittrick's bed was just plain crazy; she didn't want any more reminders of him. Against her better judgment, she stretched out and looked up at the room as a whole. With the skillful application of paint on the walls, the room had come to life. The colors brought out warm highlights in the oak headboard and blended the new look with the old. Excitement bubbled up, and she clasped her arms around her waist. Would she be pushing her luck to suggest a moss-green spread with printed pillows and a beige Berber rug?

Dream on, kiddo. She noticed Tom only reluctantly accepted things not of his own choosing. He was obviously used to having things go his way, and when they didn't, he seemed slightly off balance. He didn't roll with a punch like Raven did. Tom punched back, and that intrigued her.

Outwardly he was usually at ease, but when he wasn't in complete control, she caught the subtle signs of tension—his stiffened back, a jaw muscle that twitched, a tendency to cut her off midsentence. No doubt he was a dynamic executive, but when he *wasn't* being the boss, when he was just being a man, occasionally she detected a certain awkwardness. She couldn't help wondering why.

"Still here?" Tom's deep baritone startled her.

April gasped and scrambled off the mattress. "The room looks great, don't you think?"

Warm lights glinted in his eyes. "Yeah."

She straightened and darted a glance at him. "I was just thinking about the color scheme. You could do a lot in here, maybe color coordinate it."

The light in his eyes faded.

"Forget it. I guess it probably wouldn't interest you."

She moved toward the door, but he stepped in front of her, blocking her path. "Try me."

April swallowed. "For your bed, I was thinking. . . ."

He laughed, a low, intimate chuckle. "You like it?"

The fine hairs on the back of her neck lifted. Had he been watching her? Heat flooded her cheeks. She stared at a spot just beyond him and ran her palms down the front of her shorts. "I . . . um . . . thought a green spread might be a nice touch."

"A green spread." Amusement colored his tone.

"A soft moss green. It would add a restful feeling. And some green-and-peach print pillows scattered—"

"Too feminine."

"Oh, I don't think so. It would bring out the wall color."

His jaw tensed. "Too much trouble."

"No, it's not!" Her raised voice startled even her. She searched for a place to focus her eyes, then pinned him with her gaze. "What's wrong with decorative pillows?"

Tom frowned, and she heard his indrawn breath. "Can we talk about something else?"

Reality punched her in the chin. She'd done it again, blurted her thoughts when she should have kept her mouth shut. Why did he push all her buttons? More to the point, she thought, what did she say that pushed *his?*

"It's late. I'd better head home," she said in a low tone.

Shifting his weight from one hip to the other, he shook a wristwatch from under his shirt sleeve. "Only seven o'clock."

Their gazes met, and he looked away, but not before she saw an odd expression cross his face. "Still want your marketing lesson?"

"Of course. That was the deal—I paint, you teach."

She smoothed her hair back with her fingers, waiting for him to say something. His reserve made her nervous. Maybe he found her a thorn in his side. Well, so what if he did; a bargain was a bargain. She'd try not to upset him; surely she could manage that for the duration of her lesson.

Actually, she reflected as she stared into his troubled eyes, he managed to upset her, too. She didn't know why, it just happened. But she needed help with the computer program, so she'd just have to tough it out. With both of them on good behavior, maybe they could get through the hour in peace.

"Okay," he said at last. "I teach. I'll be over in an hour."

April was wiping the last of her dinner dishes when Tom's knock shook her door. He stood in the yellow glimmer of the porch light, a big, black binder and a yellow legal pad under one arm. He wore Levi's and a black long-sleeved T-shirt with the sleeves shoved up to his elbows. Without speaking, he strode into her living room and turned. His gaze lingered on the top button of her flannel shirt in a way that made her cheeks hot.

He shifted his attention to her face. "Ready?"

She took a deep breath. "Where would you like to start?"

"Your computer. In the workroom, right?"

"I'll bring another chair."

"I'll get it." He curled the fingers of one hand around the back of a kitchen chair and headed down the hall. April followed, a thread of apprehension crawling up her spine. There was something disturbing about the thought of sitting close to him.

The computer's blue screen glowed from the darkened

room. April snaked a hand inside the doorway and switched on the overhead light. He set the kitchen chair beside her computer, sat down, and spread his binder on the long wooden counter.

He motioned her to sit. "Where shall we start?"

"At the beginning." She hesitated. "I'm . . . um . . . not smart about some things."

"Sure fooled me. Ever used a computer before?"

"Yes, but only to write letters when Teddy was traveling."

He gave her a quick look. "Okay, let's run through the program."

April concentrated on the screen but every so often found her attention shifting to his long, tapered fingers as they touched the keys, caressed the mouse. His hands were lean and sensitive looking, made for stroking a woman's skin. She caught her breath and turned away.

He whipped his head around. "Hey, you have to watch, if you want to learn."

April sucked in a quick breath. He didn't miss a thing. "OK. The accounts receivable gets filed under income. What comes next?"

"Now you enter your customer database here, and then you call up the file when you want to promote something. It's simple, just file numbers."

"But my customers aren't numbers, they're *people*. Old Mrs. Porter, for example. She's such a sweet thing, and so poor since her husband died. I slip her an extra basket of soap when I can. Mr. Townsend gets a bottle of burdock root tincture for his arthritis, and the Jones sisters need—"

Tom clapped a hand to his forehead. "April, you're running a business, not a charity."

"I'm helping people!"

"You're going broke. Look, let's get a few things straight. The strategy to use depends on which rung you occupy on the ladder. Frankly"—he leaned forward, placing both hands on his thighs—"you don't even have your feet off the ground."

April gritted her teeth. "I'm supposed to cut off help to my customers because I'm not doing well enough? I can't do that. I couldn't sleep knowing I refused to help my friends."

Tom grimaced. "Then cut production costs. Use cheaper ingredients, other incentives. Offer them free soap or whatever, but only if they buy a certain dollar value."

"Tom, these are poor people. Neighbors. We all help each other out. They depend on me. Ignoring their needs is—is heartless."

"Business success comes from the *head,* not the heart."

She compressed her lips into a thin line. "That's mercenary."

"April, you're too soft. Mercenary is what business is *supposed* to be. You make a product, you sell it, you make money. And to do it you devise a marketing strategy. It's the law of hype."

"You're talking over my head." *And making me uncomfortable.* She crossed and uncrossed her ankles. A businessman he might be, but without concern for people.

"You create an image for your product." He gestured

with his palms out. "Even if it doesn't live up to the hype, people believe it and will buy the product."

April's temper flared. "But that's manipulative—"

"You're growing a business, April. A certain amount of marketing hype is involved in any venture. Including yours." He eyed her, a speculative look on his face. "So what if April's Garden shampoo isn't a heck of a lot different from someone else's? What's important is that you convince the public that it is."

"You mean, just *say* it's better? I don't think—"

"Not necessarily better. The marketing key is in what you imply. You can say your shampoo is handmade. That doesn't necessarily mean better, but a customer's perception is that handmade things *are* better."

"Isn't that risky? What if I'm challenged?"

He shrugged. "There's always a certain amount of risk. Comes with the territory. You risk losing a few customers who won't be getting free soap anymore, but what's important is you have the potential to gain hundreds more. The risk is worth it."

April chewed on her lower lip. She didn't want that kind of risk. She wanted to feel in touch with customers, not scrutinize a spreadsheet with numbers on it. Regardless of what he said, she didn't want to grow her business at the expense of people. Mrs. Porter would get her soap, and that was that.

Tom turned back to the computer. "When we run the numbers, you'll see I'm right."

April stared at him. He really believed this. So why was she surprised? A business executive's main interest was always numbers, not people. But not for her.

She focused on the dark hair faintly visible at his neck-band. "I think you've got it all wrong."

He hiked up his brows and studied her. "This is how business works. You're not running for Miss Congeniality, we're discussing your business strategy."

She frowned, her nerves on edge. "What about my business strategy?"

"I think you should invest in an online account. E-mail, a Web site, credit card service, and someone who'll handle your PR."

April groaned. "All that? What will it cost?"

"Around two, maybe three thousand."

She gasped. "Three thousand dollars? I just spent fifteen hundred on this computer! I can't afford that."

He sighed. "You can't afford not to. It's part of the risk, April. Part of getting your foot on that ladder rung. Without adequate funding, a product won't get off the ground." He flashed her a grin. "Marketing law number one."

April's heart clenched. If she followed his advice, she'd go broke, she just knew it. But she'd also go broke if she didn't do something to gain more customers. Talk about being between a rock and a hard place. He wouldn't be bothered by this—business risk was a part of his life. He did it every day. But for her it meant giving up her security, putting herself in danger. She squeezed her eyes shut.

Tom watched April withdraw into herself. She didn't have to say anything; her thoughts showed on her face as clearly as if they'd been penned. She was overcautious about money, about risk. He guessed she was pretty close to the wire financially, but it shouldn't matter that much if she stood to gain in the end.

Wait a minute! He'd bet something else drove her fear. Something other than money. She'd shut herself up in the cottage for what, six years? Maybe she was afraid to take chances on anything. Did she only bet on sure things?

"Look, you don't have to do everything at once. Skip the PR stuff for now. Hell, I'll build you a Web site if you'll . . . you'll help me decorate my house."

Her eyes widened. "You'd do a Web page just for my decorating help?"

Oh, God, why did he say that? He was getting used to a different lifestyle out here, but he wasn't sure he'd like all her ideas.

"You work up the database. Put down the names and addresses of everyone you've sold to, what products they bought. Then make another list of everyone you'd like to sell to—that will be your target audience. In a couple of days I'll want a list of all the products you make, and some photos."

"Photos? Of my wreaths?"

"Wreaths, lotions, whatever. And one of yourself too."

"Me? Why do you need my picture?"

"Marketing strategy. An attractive female sells merchandise. When that attractive female makes the product, all the better."

He watched her face change, guessed at the struggle going on within her.

"Scared?"

She bit her lip. "You have no idea, Tom. I feel like I did the night before Teddy and I got married."

"Yeah?" He wasn't sure he wanted to hear this.

"Yeah," she said, her voice barely audible.

Tom rose. "Growing a business is a lot like growing a relationship. You've got to reach out and try like hell."

April turned away in silence.

Tom gathered up his notepad and binder. "Lesson two tomorrow night, eight o'clock," he said in a brisk voice. "A faint heart never made much money."

Tom made his way across the meadow with mixed feelings. Her business was her problem, but he wanted to help her. Deep down he knew why: He loved a challenge, plain and simple. Over the last ten years, he'd transformed his inheritance into millions by buying failing companies, turning them around, and selling them at a profit. Even though April Fairchild's tiny herb business was an insignificant blip on the financial chart, something about her determination to succeed sparked a desire to help her.

What he really needed to do was figure out what the next step for him would be. He tramped up the front steps, through the living room, and straight into his bedroom. He shouldn't care whether she went under or not.

But he did. And that wasn't plain and simple at all.

ELEVEN

Tom headed into the kitchen, uncorked the bottle of Cabernet Sauvignon left over from his dinner, and splashed a couple inches into the chipped tumbler he'd found in the cupboard. Great wine, crummy glass. Another item for his shopping list.

He recorked the bottle, grabbed a handful of salted nuts from the can, and made his way back into the living room to settle on his grandfather's faded tan sofa. He couldn't stop thinking about April.

Her marketing naïveté surprised him. Given her sharp mind, he'd expected her to be more savvy. He popped two cashews into his mouth. Her concern for people was commendable, but in the business world, it would be her undoing.

He raised the glass to his lips and took a sip, savoring the rich, fruity taste, then leaned back against the cushion and closed his eyes. Had he ever felt as passionate about people as April did? For that matter, had he even wanted to?

The answer was no. Not for a very long time.

His grandfather had taught him well. To succeed in

business, one must divorce oneself from emotion. He'd done a good job of that, and while he'd never actually alienated anyone, neither had he gathered any friends other than Jim Rector, his attorney. And that friendship was based more on money than camaraderie.

April couldn't afford to give away her products and survive; her concern for others bordered on imprudence. And yet her generosity touched something he'd long buried. She was a caring person. He liked that. He liked other things about her, too.

Working with her, however, was a challenge he hadn't expected.

For one thing, he liked being close to her, listening to her talk about her herbs and the old roses she grew, even things as mundane as the weather or a golden sunrise. He also liked smelling the lavender-and-rose scent of her skin and hair.

Maybe her presence and the fact that she was so attractive weren't such good things. He didn't want to get close to anyone, especially a woman like her; April Fairchild was more than just a beautiful woman. The last thing he needed while he was sorting out his life was a complication.

Hold on a minute, Tom. One thing at a time. He'd solve his problem in his own way, and in the meantime he'd take care to watch himself around the long-legged flower grower. She already occupied more of his thoughts than he cared to admit.

He tossed back the rest of the wine and finished the nuts. No problem. He'd deal with April and the pull she exerted on him the way he always dealt with the unexpected—slowly and cautiously, with his emotions completely under control.

The next morning Tom padded into the kitchen in his bare feet. Sunlight slanted through the window over the kitchen sink, casting a shaft of warm golden light on the counter, and he admired the granite's speckled pattern as he made coffee in his new black coffeemaker. When it finished dripping, he grabbed the glass pot and poured a stream into a crazed red mug.

He took a sip and dragged in a lungful of the meadow-scented air. Funny how country morning sunshine and a cup of coffee could lift his spirits. Just as he reached into the refrigerator for the cream, a knock sounded at the front door.

April stood on the porch, a folder clutched in her hand. She wore a loose-fitting yellow T-shirt and faded jeans, and he tamped down a stab of disappointment, remembering the skimpy garment she'd worn yesterday, the feel of bare skin against his hand when she'd slipped off the ladder. Heat settled in his groin. He wrenched his gaze from her form and pushed the screen door open.

" 'Morning," he drawled.

"The pictures," she said. "I took these last year for the crafts fair." She thrust the folder into his hand and turned away.

"Great. I'll look them over and see you tonight."

She froze. "Tonight?"

"Lesson two, remember?"

"Yes," she breathed with a slight hesitation. Then she was gone.

Tom scanned the photos, noting the display baskets of soap and sachet, a pyramid of little blue bottles wrapped with her artistic labels. The last one was a full-figure shot of April standing in front of a tree. She wore a low-cut yellow peasant dress, and her hair curled over her shoulders in a shower of spun gold. A heart-shaped amethyst pendant nestled between her breasts, and her mouth curved in a smile that melted his heart. He found he couldn't take his eyes off the photograph.

He wanted her. His hand began to tremble, and he took a steadying breath. April Fairchild was the most beautiful woman he'd ever met, but at this moment he wished to God he'd sent her away. She spelled danger. How could he live next door to her, see her day after day, work with her, and not be affected? She was a capital D distraction.

Well, so what if she was? He'd managed "distractions" before, secretaries who threw themselves at him, business associates who were less blatant but predatory all the same. He'd wined and dined some of them, even taken a few to bed, but he'd never allowed things to get out of hand. He never lost his head, and always kept an emotional distance.

But with April? He focused on the photograph and made his way back into the kitchen. With April he wanted to talk as well as touch, and it scared the hell out of him. He grabbed his coffee mug and raised it to his lips. His lip curled; the coffee had gone cold. He wanted to get to know April, find out why she chose to hide out in the country.

He tossed the coffee into the sink, rinsed the mug, and padded to his bedroom to get his shoes.

* * *

At eight o'clock Tom took a fortifying breath and rapped on April's door. He'd spent the better part of the afternoon trying to decide if he wanted to see her or not.

"It's open," her voice echoed from inside.

He strode in and found her at the kitchen table, writing. Loose papers littered the surface. She looked up and tucked them in a notebook.

"How's it going?" he asked, working to keep his voice casual. She'd changed into a black knit jumper and white fitted top that showed off her tiny waist and slim hips. His pulse throbbed.

She stood up. "Okay, I guess. I'm ready."

Tom nodded. "Working on your customer list?"

She tapped the blue spiral notebook. "Customer list, wish list of everyone I wish was a customer."

He picked it up, skimmed the pages, then looked at her hard. "There are only ninety-six names on this list."

Her eyes widened. "That's everyone I could think of."

He chucked the notebook onto the table. "You'll never get there by shortchanging yourself. Marketing is a battle of perceptions—and the first skirmish is in the mind, not in the marketplace."

April groaned. "That sounds like English, but I don't understand a word you're saying."

Tom exhaled with a *whoosh*. "You have to create the illusion of success. One way is with mass mailing, and"—he focused on her eyes, noting her bewildered expression—"you're going to need a hell of a lot bigger list than this. And you'll need to impress every person on the list, make them believe you have something they need, something that thousands of others buy regularly."

A furrow etched her forehead. "But that wouldn't be truthful."

"Truth is nothing more than one expert's perception." Eyeing her intently, he leaned closer. "You happen to be that expert."

Her mouth thinned. "I refuse to be dishonest. Besides, I only know so many people."

"So send mailings to people you don't know." He pushed his fingers through his hair. "Look," he said wearily, "no one's saying you are dishonest. You have to create a prosperous image, even if it's not exactly the case. It's the way marketing is done every day."

He began to pace the area between the kitchen and the front door, trying to figure out what to say to her. She looked terribly vulnerable with her rounded eyes and creased brow. What he really wanted to do was gather her in his arms and kiss her. Not a good idea, he reminded himself. He took a minute to gather his thoughts.

"Good marketing depends on a carefully crafted illusion."

Her eyes flashed. "Not at the expense of my customers. I won't do it."

He stopped his pacing three feet in front of her. "Then what will you do?" he asked quietly. "You want your business to survive. What are you willing to do?"

"I need more customers, I understand that. But I won't lie to the ones I have. I need your help, but I can't do this if I lose my self-respect."

The concern in her eyes cut straight to his heart. Why in God's name was this so difficult? Why did he care whether her flower sachets sold well?

He didn't know why. All he knew was that four days

ago he wanted her gone, and now it mattered to him whether her business went under. Whether *she* went under.

The why question, he acknowledged, was moot. He did care. When had he started to? He stood very still, watching her fidget with her pencil. Not only was she vulnerable, she was defensive. Rather like one of her cats, protecting its territory.

She glanced up at him from the chair, her mouth beginning to tremble. "I think we'd better—"

"All right," Tom said. "We'll do it your way. But try to keep a rein on your generosity. Too many customer freebies will deplete your entire stock."

He handed her the customer list and reached for a chair. When it didn't budge, he gave it a yank. A large orange cat leaped onto the floor, sniffed his trouser leg, then sashayed indignantly over to the sofa.

April pushed her chair back and got to her feet. Her pulse pounded, but whether from anger or something else she couldn't tell. Why did he make her feel so uneasy? It made no sense. At least she'd made her point.

She allowed herself a brief inspection of Tom's rangy form. His hair, still damp from the shower, flopped onto his forehead, the ends waving. His eyes were the same moss green as the turtleneck he wore. Cashmere, she guessed, tucked casually into indigo denims. She longed to touch it, and the muscles beneath. The spicy musk scent of his aftershave made her heartbeat quicken. She stepped back.

"Shall we create that database?" he asked.

She nodded. Turning on her heel, she made her way toward the computer in her workroom.

By the time she keyed in the last name on her list, an hour had passed. Once he'd shown her how to use the program, all it took was concentration. She had to work to keep her eyes on the list and not on his hands or any other part of him. While she worked, he made notes or looked over her shoulder at the screen. Once, she stole a glance at his face and found him watching her. She jerked her gaze back to the screen and inadvertently deleted an entire page.

"I'm finished," she announced at last.

"Not quite." He handed her a page of notes. "I need a description of each type of sachet—what's in them, why they're the best. Same for the soap and whatever else you sell. Write a paragraph and I'll rework it for the Web page."

He reached out a hand toward her arm, then dropped it. The gesture sent a sizzle up her spine. He was going to touch her! For an instant, she felt a flicker of sadness when he did not.

"Don't worry about being effervescent," he said with a trace of something she could not define. "I'll handle that part."

"But I can't write anything that's not true."

"It will all be true, just"—he drew in a quick breath— "embellished. April, you're trying to convince a new customer base that your product is the one they can't do without. You've got to *advertise* the product."

He handed her his notes and stood. "I've jotted down what I need here. The sooner you get it to me, the sooner I can put it online." He started for the door.

She rose and followed him. "It's not that I'm not interested in marketing. I just question your tactics. It's because. . . ." Her voice trailed off.

How could she tell him exactly what she felt? How could she admit she was afraid and not have to explain herself? He was so assured, so matter-of-fact about everything. But he was a numbers man, and she was a people person. They were like night and day.

"I understand what you're saying. Probably what you aren't saying too. Don't worry, April." He cupped her chin between his thumb and forefinger and gave her a look that curled her toes. "It's not my intent to make you do anything you don't want to do."

But you already are. You're making me want to touch you, feel your arms around me. She pulled away and opened the door. Shadow darted between their feet and made a beeline for the bowl of kibble beside the refrigerator.

Tom gave her an odd look. "I thought you said you only had nine cats."

"I do."

"Can you really keep track of how many there are? What keeps them from reproducing?"

"Just good sense. They're all fixed."

Tom chuckled. "Kinda takes their fun away, doesn't it?"

"Fun?"

"You know, sex. Mating."

Heat made her cheeks burn. "I try not to think about it."

"And are you successful?" His gaze locked with hers.

"No," she said without thinking. "I mean, yes. Yes, I am."

He moved closer. "You know, I don't think I believe you."

April stepped back and found herself next to the bookcase. "You don't?" Her voice came out a whisper, and she sidestepped, putting the chair between them.

"No. But we'll pursue this another time." He stepped to the door and closed it behind him.

The sound of his footsteps faded as he made his way across the meadow.

She traced the path his fingers had made, then cupped her face in her hands. It was easier when they were adversaries, with the hostility between them barely concealed. It had been easy enough to dislike the Tom McKittrick who threatened to evict her from her home. But this Tom was different, especially when his eyes softened and his low voice rolled over her like warm honey.

So he's not the ogre you thought he was at first. He's a nice guy. A bit out of place up here but he was trying. The trick was not to notice his eyes and his voice and that male scent that sent her blood thrumming.

She didn't need it. Him.

But, oh, Lord, she wanted it anyway.

TWELVE

April tossed a final scoop of black compost onto her wheelbarrow, anchored her shovel on top, then grabbed the handles and staggered toward the center of the meadow where a freshly dug rosebed awaited. She slowed to gaze at the old roses growing between her cottage and the main house. A Jacques Cartier with its cupped pink petals hugged the ground. Behind it a bold pink Madame Isaac Pereire gave off an intense damask fragrance that stopped her in her tracks.

She closed her eyes for an instant to savor the rich perfumed air, then rested her gaze on a Dorothy Perkins clambering over a stretch of weathered fence that bordered the cottage yard. Covered in blooms in shades of palest pink to a vibrant rose, the old rambler was one of her favorites. She'd rescued the neglected bush from the yard of an old Victorian torn down to make room for the town's firehouse. The rose had flourished, and it sparked her interest in propagating other roses at Creggan.

She gave the wheelbarrow handles a shove. Time was wasting, and she had work to do on her business plan after she finished composting the new rose bed. As the barrow bumped clumsily along the grassy tufts, she struggled to keep the mounded load from toppling. This was the second year she'd amended the soil using her kelp mixture; despite its fishy smell, she enjoyed the task.

Nourishing living things made her feel good deep down, and running her hands through the rich earth was even more sensual than breathing in the fragrance of the full-blown rose blossoms. Last year's blooms were the most breathtaking she'd produced, and to her surprise, she won two ribbons at the Sonoma County fair. Now, with her newest cuttings rooted and ready to plant, she was one step closer to completing her landscaping plan for the meadow.

She gazed at the lath arbor tucked neatly into a corner between the rose hedge and the cultivated square of antique roses, its structure nearly obscured by the profusely blooming New Dawn. A trio of Portland roses, heavy with buds, flanked each side and grew up around the back of the slat bench. When Tom saw the roses in full bloom, he'd be glad he let her stay. Grounds like Creggan needed expert maintenance. Besides, her work in the gardens was intrinsically satisfying.

She stepped over a grassy tussock and the wheel suddenly sank into mire, pitching the wheelbarrow forward when its load shifted. She tugged on the handles, but it wouldn't budge.

Lord, of all the times to get stuck! She had troubles enough getting her chores done without this. She hated to ask for help, but maybe Tom could give her a hand.

She glanced up at the main house. The painters were back. The Fahy white panel truck sat alongside Tom's silver Mercedes, and figures in white coveralls carried equipment up the front steps, but there was no sign of Tom.

She stared at the wheelbarrow. Maybe if she put all her weight behind it. . . . She tightened her grip on the wooden handles. "One, two," she counted under her breath. "Thr—"

Without warning, her smooth-soled sneakers slipped on the damp grass and her bottom smacked onto the ground. "Hell and damnation," she muttered. Her buttocks stung from the impact, and her legs felt shaky. She struggled to get up.

Tom materialized from behind her. "Allow me." Grasping her arms, he pulled her to her feet. Twin lines of concern marched up the bridge of his nose. "You all right?"

She wasn't sure. With his arms around her, her pulse pounded in her ears. "My . . . pride is bruised," she said, her voice uneven.

His eyes twinkled. "That and something else, I'll bet."

She slipped out of his grip and brushed off the seat of her denim shorts. Her arms tingled where his fingers had rested.

He clamped both hands around the wheelbarrow handles and jockeyed it out of the mud. "Where were you going with this?"

She pointed to a verdigris statue of a peasant girl in the center of the meadow and the circular bed she'd dug around it. "Over there, by the statue."

He gazed at the prepared ground and started forward, pushing the wheelbarrow ahead of him. A fresh breeze sprang up, rustling the leaves in the sycamore trees. Tom sniffed the air and made a face. "Good God, what is this stuff?"

"Compost. I make it from kelp."

He wrinkled his nose. "Kelp smells like this?"

She removed one glove and wiped her damp palm on her shorts. "Plus a little steer manure and fish emulsion."

"Pretty disgusting stuff." He halted the barrow beside the freshly turned earth.

"Yes, it smells awful, but it's worth it." She scooped up a handful of the compost and held it out to him. "It's very good for roses." She let the mixture sift through her fingers onto the new bed.

He focused on her, his eyes reflecting the green of the meadow. "You don't mind working with this stuff?"

"No, why should I? It doesn't bother me to get my hands dirty."

He hesitated a moment. "You . . . uh . . . don't seem like the type to sort through this muck."

"It's not muck. It's good rich compost. Besides, I'm used to it. I've been doing this for the last six years."

Tom drew his brows together. "I seem to recall your mentioning a town house back east and hired help."

"What does that have to do with anything? I used to spend summers with my grandma in North Adams. She had a huge garden." April smiled, remembering sunny summer days and picking wild strawberries.

"Grandma taught me to make compost. She had a big U-shaped bin with removable slats at one end." She tossed her hair back over her shoulders. "The very first time I tried to open the gate, I climbed up and fell head-first into the bin. Grandma had to hose me off before she'd let me in the house."

Tom grinned. "That sounds like fun," he said, his tone wry.

"It was, really. Grandma let me run free, something my parents never allowed. She called me her little hooligan." April glanced down at her grass-stained shorts, scraped knee. "Guess I haven't changed much."

A flame flickered in his eyes. "I'd say you've changed a great deal."

April's cheeks warmed, and a long moment passed. The way he looked at her, letting his gaze linger over her body, made her throat tighten. She didn't like him studying her. Well, maybe she did, deep down. But, even so, it made her nervous. She wondered what she looked like in his eyes.

He propped his arms on the shovel and stared at her. "You're full of surprises, you know that? I figured being the wife of a jet-setter like Teddy Fairchild, you lived in a penthouse with thick, white carpets. Now you tell me you like grubbing in the dirt."

She stiffened. "I lived in Teddy's world, but I didn't belong there."

One dark eyebrow arched. "Kinda defensive, aren't you? All I said was—"

"I know what you said." Her sharp tone surprised even her. "You're stereotyping me. Teddy used to do that, and it made me crazy. I won't be put in a box."

He raised the other brow. "Is that why you left? He pinned labels on you? Why didn't you fight back?"

"What makes you think I didn't?" She grabbed the handles of the wheelbarrow, turned it on its side, and spilled the entire load onto the rose bed. Then she knelt and began to spread it evenly with her hands. "Teddy called me his 'little woman.' Or his 'sex goddess,' depending on his mood. He never saw beneath the roles. He thought all women played roles."

Tom said nothing, but she knew he watched her. She swallowed and listened to the steady hum of bees circling the rose blossoms. When she could stand it no longer, she turned her head and looked up at him. His eyes burned into hers. "It's a moot point now. Teddy's dead."

"It's important if it made you run away."

"I didn't." She turned away, the old guilt welling up. "I left him. That's not running away."

His eyes told her he didn't believe her. "I think you ran clear across the country to get away from something. Maybe you're still running away, April."

"I came here, I liked it, I stayed. I am not running away. End of story."

"End of chapter, maybe. I'll bet it isn't the end of the story."

His cocksure attitude raised the hackles on her neck. It was one thing to be curious about her, but he was pushing her dangerously close to things she didn't want to think about. She had to change the subject.

Scrambling to her feet, she righted the wheelbarrow. "You got my write-up on the sachets and soap?"

"Found it stuffed in the screen door this morning."

"Well," she said, clasping her arms around her waist. "Was it all right?"

He gave her a quick smile. "You'll hardly recognize your product by the time I'm finished with the rewrite."

She hesitated. "Wait a minute. I don't like fancy descriptions; they're not accurate. You said—"

"I said we'd be truthful, and we will." He set the

shovel back in the wheelbarrow and turned to her. "You said you wanted to develop a marketing plan. This is the way you do that."

"But—"

"I've been doing this for fifteen years. I know what will make it work. Trust me."

Trust him? A smooth, good-looking guy with the same flair for sweet-talking that Teddy had? Not on her life. "I, um. . . ."

"April, what are you afraid of?" He paced back and forth between the rose hedge and the statue, stopping five feet from her. "You're a business person who wants to survive. You have got to take the initiative. Be aggressive. Are you scared to move beyond the little fortress you've built here?"

"It's not a fortress. It's my home."

"It's your business, too. But it's hidden away."

"So what? Lots of people run businesses from home. Look at Ben and Jerry."

"Ben and Jerry advertise. A lot. They get the word out. You'll never grow your business unless you do the same."

"I like it just fine the way it is—small and personal. I don't want to change that."

"But you're going under."

She gulped. "I'm going under," she acknowledged with a sigh.

He took a step closer. "The other day you accused me of not wanting to change over something as mundane as paint. Isn't this the same? You're so fearful of change, I can hardly convince you to help yourself."

A king-size lump lodged in her throat. He had no right

to talk to her like this. She was surprised that the things he said were so hurtful. Tears stung her eyes, but she'd be damned if she'd cry.

"You don't know what you're talking about." Her throat closed, and she stalked off toward the pond.

"You're doing it again," he called after her. "Running away."

Damn him. Damn him to hell. She slipped behind the rose hedge and made her way along the stepping stones to the edge of the meadow and the enclosed pond garden. She dropped to her knees and sat facing the water.

Men like Tom were part of the reason she was here. Men to whom people were dealt with as numbers to be manipulated and not human beings with unique needs. She lived here because it was where she could be herself. Not a figurehead or trophy wife. *Herself.*

She splashed water on her face and dried it with the hem of her plaid work shirt. Teddy had thought her sole purpose in life was to look beautiful and make him happy. While he gallivanted around the world in pursuit of pleasure, he'd expected her to stay home and wait for him. She'd had to leave him or shrivel up inside. She would never give up her independence for anyone again.

April rubbed her eyes with her fists. Freedom to make her own choices, to be herself was the most important thing in the world. Without that she might just as well be dead and buried like Teddy.

She had made the same mistake with Teddy that her mother had with her father. They had both married charming, willful men who treated them like storybook dolls, not real people. Tom and Teddy were one and the same, and one bad experience was enough for a lifetime.

As if she'd conjured him up by her thoughts, Tom dropped down behind her. "April," he said in a husky voice. He slid alongside her so she was forced to look at him. Pain laced his green-brown eyes. "I shouldn't have said you were running away."

She sat very still, her hands folded in her lap. The scream of a red-tailed hawk broke the stillness. Its long broad wings formed a shallow *v* as it swooped low in the meadow, then soared skyward again. April envied its mastery of the air.

"What is it you're afraid of?" He placed one hand on her shoulder. The other he laid over her hands. "Can I help?"

She looked away. "You can leave me alone."

He continued staring at her, his eyes turning smoky brown. His Adam's apple bobbed. "I don't believe that's what you want."

She didn't answer. Her hand shook, and his fingers tightened around hers.

"Say it. Tell me you want me to go."

"I don't know what I want anymore. It's all a muddle."

"I'm feeling a lot of that myself." He raised his hand and tilted her chin. "Look at me, April." He lifted her chin a fraction so she gazed into his eyes. "This may not be the time, but I want to kiss you."

He lowered his head slightly, and she felt the soft heat of his breath on her face. Warmth spread through her belly. She rimmed her lower lip with her tongue.

"I've wanted to kiss you since the day you slipped off that ladder," he murmured, his low voice a caress. "And I think you want me to."

"This is crazy. I don't want you to kiss me. I've forgotten all about that episode at the ladder."

But she hadn't. She remembered every detail, the way his eyes changed to a smoky green when he held her close, the feather-soft feel of his lips on hers, even the heat of his hands on her arms. If she was truthful, she'd have to admit she *did* want him to kiss her. Oh, yes, she most definitely did.

Her heart tripped, and she waited, parting her lips to tell him. Then his mouth came down hard on hers. He leaned forward and pulled her against him, his heart beating so loudly she could hear it. Or was it her own?

April found her arms encircling him as if they had a mind of their own. She opened her mouth and he dipped his tongue inside. Heat spread in her chest, flowed like fire in her veins. Her stomach catapulted.

He groaned, deepening the kiss.

Her thighs clenched, and her breath stopped.

A thought drifted into her mind, and suddenly she broke free. It was one thing to kiss Tom and another to follow where it would lead—making love. And if she did that . . . if she made love with him, she would care about him, and that was a recipe for disaster. Having feelings for a man would threaten her independence. Reluctantly, she moved out of his embrace.

"I think we should keep our relationship strictly business."

He gave her a brief, surprised look, but she could see the heaving of his chest, his dilated pupils. Desire radiated from his body.

He closed his eyes and seemed to gather resolve from a deep breath. "I think so, too. I didn't plan this, but now that it's happened, it's plain there's a chemistry between us."

He got to his feet, reached a hand to help her up, then closed his fingers on her shoulders. Their gazes locked. "I'll tell you straight out that I want you, April."

She crossed her arms. "Well, I don't want you back."

He grinned. "You're a lousy liar, you know that?"

"OK, I'm a liar." She gave him a long look. "You're attractive, sexy, even. But you're just exactly what I don't need." Without a backward glance, she spun away and set off down the path that cut through the grass toward her cottage.

Tom groaned. He knew she wanted him. Her response to him damn near curled his toes. But she was afraid of something.

He ran shaking fingers through his hair. When he came up here for the summer, he'd needed to get himself together. Absolutely no stress, Dr. Martin had said. Now that his company had been sold, one question had been answered, but the issue was deeper than where his next job would be. He had to decide what he believed was worth doing with the rest of his life. He'd come to the country for peace and quiet so he could think things out; now he wondered if he could do that with a distraction like April around.

He stared at her retreating figure. His suggestion that she was running from something had been a shot in the dark, but from her reaction he guessed he'd hit the nail on the head. Maybe it had something to do with Teddy, her husband.

Well, he wasn't Teddy, he was Tom. He didn't want her to run from him. On the other hand, maybe he did.

There was no real future for the two of them; they were as different as night and day. She'd never want to fit into his world; she'd already been there and didn't like it. And he sure as hell didn't fit into hers.

He tramped back to the house. Damn it anyway. Why did he feel like he'd been punched in the gut?

He and the gorgeous flower grower had to talk.

THIRTEEN

April grabbed the wheelbarrow, then trundled it across the yard to her toolshed. Her mind churned, and a tension headache hammered her temple.

Tom McKittrick asked questions she couldn't answer. Was she running away? God knew she didn't want to think how hard it had been to leave Teddy, and she'd suffered over his death. She'd already packed her car and set out across the country when the news of his accident came. She didn't stop until she reached Lupine Valley.

Tom said other things that disturbed her, did things she didn't want to think about. His kiss was one of them, she acknowledged. She'd wanted Tom to touch her, hold her, and now that he had, she knew two things about him that she hadn't been aware of before. He was a very perceptive man, and she liked being kissed by him. She liked it so much she couldn't let it happen again.

Getting close to Tom McKittrick was dangerous. She'd struggled hard to find her real self, and she'd based her life on it. She wasn't going to throw it away. She'd felt suffocated by Teddy, and Tom had similar tendencies—he liked to take over a project, and he liked to run it his way. Tom's values might be admirable, but he was a high-powered executive, a manipulator. He cared about numbers, not people.

She latched the toolshed and climbed the front steps to her door, her jaw so tense it made her throat ache. Tom posed the same threat Teddy had.

Inside, she plugged in the electric kettle. Shadow hopped up in her chair, demanding attention, and she idly stroked the cat's soft black fur and waited for the water to heat.

For six years she'd managed by herself, had needed no one to help her survive. The funny part was she hadn't been lonely. But now Tom was here and things felt different.

Since she'd come to Creggan she hadn't even thought about another man or the possibility of another relationship. Her life as a single woman was just fine, just the way she wanted it.

Wasn't it? She closed her eyes and rested her elbows on the countertop. Tom's kisses made her want things. Companionship and fulfillment. Intimacy. He appealed to her on a deeper level, one that touched her mind as well as her body.

The kettle whistled. Straightening, she absentmindedly dropped a peppermint tea bag into her favorite green mug, leaned over, and unplugged the kettle. Without thinking, she poured out boiling water, carried the mug into the living room, and curled up in the red leather chair.

She had two batches of lavender and oatmeal soap waiting to be cut and wrapped for the farmers' market tomorrow, three dozen sachet bags to fill, and twenty-four tea rose cuttings to plant. But all she wanted to do was close her eyes and remember the taste of Tom's mouth on hers.

She sipped the strong tea and stared at the photograph of Teddy on the bookshelf. He'd been handsome and charming, and it had been so romantic when they had eloped. But their real life together was a jolt. He treated her like a Barbie doll, pampered her with expensive clothes, but he never listened to her, never had time to care about her needs.

It had taken all her courage to walk away from Teddy, and she'd done it with both eyes open. She'd given up her sham marriage, but she'd won herself. Even though she felt terrible when Teddy was killed, she knew she could never go back to being just a possession again.

The ring of the telephone roused Tom from his floor sanding. He got to his feet, felt a sharp twinge in his right knee, and staggered over to the telephone on the desk in his office. "McKittrick."

"Where the hell you been, Tommy boy?"

Tom's jaw tightened. Jim Rector was the only person who called him Tommy, and he never did it unless he wanted something. "I'm up to my ass in sandpaper," he told the attorney.

"Damn it, man, I've been trying to reach you for two days. You turn off your cell phone?"

"I've been busy." Tom rested the receiver on his shoulder.

"Aren't we all? If you hadn't left your phone number

with my secretary, I'd still be wondering where you disappeared to. How's the place?"

Tom sighed. "Heck of a lot better than when I arrived, no thanks to you. If it hadn't been for Mrs. Fairchild, I would've been sleeping in my car."

"What do you mean? She's supposed to be gone."

"She's still here. I—we came to an agreement."

A long silence ensued, broken by the striking of a match. Jim lighting one of his Havana cigars. "Get rid of her," the voice on the other end of the line said after a moment.

"I can't. Not now."

"Whaddya mean 'not now'?" Rector's voice rose. "That woman has been getting a free ride long enough. I can't believe you didn't kick her out."

"Hold on a minute." Tom felt his blood pressure rise. "She pays rent."

Rector gave a nasty chuckle. "Peanuts, Tommy boy. The broad hoodwinked your grandfather into signing a lease that practically gave her the property. Looks like I'll have to come up and set you—and her—straight."

"Easy, Jim," Tom said, trying to keep a lid on his temper. "You don't know the whole story. She—" The phone clicked.

Tom swore under his breath. If Jim Rector weren't the best attorney west of the Rockies, he'd fire him, friend or not. He pushed too hard. The man had a lump of coal for a heart.

Tom punched in the attorney's number and got a busy signal. He plunked the receiver back on its cradle. Just what he intended to tell Jim, he didn't exactly know; he liked having April around, that was one thing. And the other thing was that it was none of Jim's business what his reasons might be. Jim had a surprise coming. He, not his attorney, ran his life, and the sooner Jim learned that, the better.

Tom glanced at the wood shavings on the floor. The sanding could wait. He needed some fresh air.

April parked her car at the cottage door and carried the two empty wicker baskets inside. Not only had she sold all her sachets at the farmers' market, but she'd distributed the one hundred flyers Tom had designed describing her products and the new Web site, which he said would be up and running today.

She slipped out of her denim dress and hung it in the closet, passing the full-length mirror on the closet door. Usually she was too busy to give herself more than a cursory glance, but today she paused in front of the glass and slid her palms down her body. The white cotton panties and plain bra were functional but not decorative. The baby fat she'd carried when she and Teddy married had melted away, and in its place the mirror showed a flat tummy and tan, muscular legs. Tom often studied them, she acknowledged. She wondered if he would like the rest of her?

Her hands stilled. *Don't think about it.* She shook her head and moved away from the mirror to her dresser. Tom invaded too many of her thoughts lately.

Fishing a pale-yellow T-shirt from the drawer, she paired it with a clean pair of jeans, then searched in the closet and found her yellow-and-gray-plaid flannel shirt. Even though the temperature was warm, she needed the shirt to protect her arms from thorns; as she pulled it on she couldn't help thinking how Tom's hands had felt on her skin.

On her way outside she took an apple from the fruit basket on the counter to quell her rumbling stomach. She'd been too busy to stop for lunch, had kept herself purposely on the move to avoid thinking about Tom and those unguarded moments when his eyes probed beneath the layers she kept carefully hidden.

It took two trips with the wheelbarrow to get all twenty-four plastic containers of potted roses out to the newly prepared bed. When she had set out all the new pots and arranged and rearranged them in a pleasing mix of height and color, she plunged her shovel into the black earth and dug the first hole. An explicable contentment settled over her. It always did when she added something new to the landscape, but today the feeling was marred by her troubled thoughts.

She directed her mind to the task at hand. She'd found the verdigris statue of the eighteenth-century peasant girl years ago when she was looking for clay pots, but until now she'd never come up with a design that complemented it. Now, she knew exactly what she wanted: a bower of roses surrounding the base.

She dropped to her knees, knocked the root ball out of the container, and gently set the rose into the prepared hole. Then with her hands she scooped in handfuls of soil until the hole was filled. Soil particles clung to her fingers, and the sun's penetrating heat warmed her back. A hummingbird hovered over the statue, investigating the rose foliage.

She sighed as her tight neck muscles began to relax.

Creggan was the most peaceful spot on earth. She didn't ever want to leave.

"Grubbing in the dirt again?" Tom's voice broke into her thoughts.

She tamped the soil around the base of the rose but didn't look up. "That's what it takes to grow flowers."

He strode over until he stood four feet from her. "I've got your new Web site online. I thought you might like to see it."

She had to crane her neck to look up at him. He'd been working; a film of sawdust coated the knees of his jeans. He wore a green, cotton shirt, unbuttoned at the top, the tails loosely tucked in at his waist. Even in his work clothes, he looked like a *Gentlemen's Quarterly* model. And just thinking about his wavy silvered hair made her fingers itch to run them through it.

She wrenched her gaze back to the twenty-three pots waiting to be planted and squared her shoulders. "I have to finish here."

"More roses? There must be hundreds of them here already!"

"These are my own cuttings. They'll look wonderful in their own special plot." She reached for the shovel.

Tom curled his fingers around the handle. "Let me do it."

"I can manage it myself. Besides, why would you want to do this? I'll bet you've never had a shovel in your hands before."

"True. I don't know why, exactly. Just . . . been restless lately." He frowned. The hitch in his voice made her wonder if he wasn't struggling with something.

"Got some things to work out," he said. "Sometimes

it helps to do something physical. In the city I played racquetball, out here I might as well dig a few ditches."

"Holes, not ditches."

"Whatever. It'll feel good to get my body moving. Show me where to dig." He pried the shovel from her hands. "You said you'd teach me about this kind of life. How about a lesson now?"

Mirth bubbled up, but she forced her lips into a thin line. "You asked me to teach you about country living. You don't need to plant roses for survival."

He gave her a smile that left her breathless. "No, but the job will go faster if we both work at it." He moved a pot and stabbed the tip of the shovel into the earth where she pointed. He dug three holes in succession, then knelt down beside her, clamping both hands around a container. "Now what?"

He sounded eager, but behind his lighthearted words she sensed a tension. Something told her he needed to do this. She rolled the container on its side to loosen the soil, then pulled it away from the plant. "Be careful not to disturb the root ball," she cautioned.

He took the rose from her and settled it in the hole. Then he began to push in the adjacent dirt with his hands.

"Wait." She gripped his hand to stop him. "Turn the plant so the new growth faces outward." She leaned forward, grasped the plant and began to rotate it. Suddenly he reached into the hole and placed his hands over hers. His fingers shook.

Her heart leapt, but she held herself still. He gave the rose a quarter turn. "Like this?" His hands lingered on hers.

She lifted her fingers away. "Tamp it down gently,"

she said, her voice strained. "Keep the soil below the crown." She pointed to the swelling at the base.

They worked for two hours, side by side, saying little, but April felt his tension, and her heart caught. He was troubled by something. She wanted to help, but she hadn't a clue what was wrong.

After they planted the last rose, Tom stood up and groaned. "My back's never going to be the same." He reached for her hand and helped her to her feet. Their eyes met and held. For just an instant, the cloud lifted, and a warmth she hadn't seen before shone from his eyes.

Her heartbeat quickening, she jerked her gaze away and stepped back to look over the new garden plot. "What do you think?"

He moved to stand beside her and gave it, and then her, a critical squint. "I think you look very beautiful with dirt on your nose."

She swiped at her nose with the back of a forefinger, then brushed dirt off her jeans and forced herself to scrutinize the bronzy figurine atop its two-foot pillar. "I found the statue in a box in the toolshed," she said, desperate to change the subject. Her pulse hammered erratically. "I think your grandfather bought it but never found the right spot for it. It looks just right here between the pond and the old roses."

Tom inclined his head toward April, his face an odd mix of curiosity and regret. When she met his gaze, he looked away. "My grandfather was never interested in gardening when I knew him. Guess he changed."

"He did love these gardens," she said carefully. "He told me about wanting the pond, so I made that my first project, to thank him for letting me live here." She tossed her hair back on her shoulders. "I try to plant things he would have wanted."

"Is that why you work so hard? Because of him?"

"The gardening? I do it for me. After all, it's my livelihood. Your grandfather would be pleased, but this"—she spread her hand in a circle that encompassed the meadow—"this also pleases me."

He followed the motion of her hand, then brought his focus back to her. His eyes reflected an intensity she found disconcerting. He seemed to say one thing and be thinking another.

"I patterned my whole life after Grandfather's, studied at his alma mater, ran my companies the way he taught me. I even bought the same stocks he did." He sighed. "I wish I'd seen this side of him when I was growing up."

"Would it have made a difference?"

Tom clasped and unclasped his hands. A veil dropped over his features. "Two months ago I'd have said no. Now. . . ." His voice trailed off, and he swallowed. "Now, I'm trying to see things differently."

April squinted into the fading sun, wondering why the sudden throaty quality of Tom's voice made her pulse jump. "I think your grandfather reevaluated his life after he got here, and decided he needed a lot more than money. More than mere success."

Tom's face hardened. " 'Mere success'? What do you mean by that? Success is the measure of a man's worth. If he hasn't got that, he doesn't have much."

"Oh, Tom, success isn't what's important. If you work hard just to be successful or rich but you aren't happy, then it's a pretty hollow victory, isn't it?"

He frowned. "What about yourself? You're having a helluva time struggling to survive up here."

She gave him a half smile. "Sure, I'm struggling. At first it was awful. It was hard to get used to the quiet, and it was very scary to be entirely dependent on the land. I learned a lot that first year. I had to decide what was important to me. But you know what? Now, I sleep easy at night and wake up at peace just because I'm alive. I don't have much money, but I feel fulfilled."

"Are you really?" His eyes probed hers. "I wonder."

FOURTEEN

April turned her garden gloves over and examined the stitching. Two weeks ago she would have defended her statement, but now there was an element of doubt. Being fulfilled meant one's needs were met, and in her case that wasn't entirely accurate. True, she was concerned about her financial affairs, but now she was aware of another, more disturbing element of her life.

For the first time in six years, she felt lonely.

She kept her eyes averted. "Let's talk about something else. The Web site?"

He wiped his forehead with the back of his hand. "I want you to see it, but it's getting late. Tell you what, I'll throw on a couple of steaks, and you can look at the site while they're cooking."

April's lids snapped open. "No, I—I don't think so. Not tonight."

"Why not? You have to eat, too. This way you won't have to cook. Besides"—he gave her a boyish smile and clasped his hands over his midsection—"all that gardening makes me ravenous."

He had a point. She too was hungry. But she had so

much to do; between now and Tuesday she had to make two batches of lavender soap and stitch four dozen new sachet bags. If she opened a can of tuna for dinner, she could lay out the material and start cutting while she ate.

And that way you won't have sexy Mr. Tom McKittrick across the table from you, asking questions, making you think about how lonely you are.

April laughed out loud. She raised her palms, then let them fall at her sides. Who was she kidding? Tom McKittrick occupied her thoughts whether or not he was across the table from her.

"Come by just for a minute and have a look at the Web page. I don't want to put up anything you're not happy with."

"Well, maybe . . . just for a minute," she heard herself say.

Tom grinned and started across the meadow, taking such long strides April had to stretch her legs to keep up. She told herself she'd peek at the page and then head for home. "I think—"

She jerked when a ringing telephone interrupted. Without breaking stride, Tom pulled his cell phone from his shirt pocket.

"McKittrick. Yeah, I've heard of it. Manufactures digital recorders, diagnostic equipment." He marched up the front porch steps, motioning April inside.

"Is that right? It's interesting, but fifty-one percent or it's no go. . . . No, I don't care that he—"

"You're busy. I won't stay," April mouthed. She turned to go, but Tom reached out and grabbed her wrist. "Not long," he said with his free hand covering the receiver.

"What's that? No, Carl, I'm busy. We'll talk in the

morning. . . . Doing? I'm"—he grinned at April—"in the middle of dinner." His expression suddenly intense, he whispered, "Don't go."

"No, not alone," he told the caller.

He looked at April, an amused expression in his eyes. "Yes, she's attractive. . . . Right, Carl. I'm a pretty good judge of that."

While Tom talked, April glanced into the living room and gasped. The drapes had been stripped from the windows, the sofa and three chairs sat in a corner, covered with canvas drop cloths, and the once dingy room now sparkled with a fresh coat of buff-colored paint.

"Yeah, sure, Carl," Tom said into the receiver. "First thing in the morning. Tell Jim I'll work on it." He switched the phone off and stuffed it in his pocket, then gestured at the living room. "Like it?" he asked.

"Yes, actually. I'm surprised it's not white. You said you paint everything white."

He shrugged. "Seemed like a good time to try something new." He sent her a controlled look, his eyes distant. "I can change my mind, April."

He led her through the room into what she remembered as the library. It looked completely different. In place of the faded carpet was a half-stripped oak floor covered with a fine layer of sawdust. *Tom must be doing the sanding himself,* she thought. That accounted for the sawdust on his knees.

She glanced at the walls covered in the same buff shade as the living room. Even the empty oak bookcases looked as if they'd been cleaned and waxed. She had to give him credit for experimenting. Maybe he wasn't as rigid as he'd seemed at first.

In place of Jerome McKittrick's worn mahogany desk sat a new executive-size one in golden oak; behind it she spied a matching computer workstation with a shelf unit filled with manuals and boxes of software. Next to a laptop computer, scanner, and printer were a copier and a fax machine.

"My new office," Tom said, waving a hand at the arrangement.

April ran her fingers over the hand-rubbed desk. He sure didn't waste time. "I thought you came here to rest."

"I don't like hanging in limbo," he said, turning on the computer. "I've always had a number of projects in the works."

"What sort of projects?"

"Buying companies in trouble, mergers, that sort of thing."

He keyed in a command, and she watched the brilliant blue of the screen's desktop emerge.

"Did Carl have a prospect for you?"

"He did. A manufacturer of digital equipment. They're overextended and are going belly up. But I'm not interested."

"Why not?"

Tom hesitated. "Well, actually, I'm deciding whether I want to continue doing this."

"Are you good at it?"

"Yes. But that's not the problem. I'm not sure I like doing it anymore. It used to give me a real adrenaline rush to turn a company around; the last couple of years I haven't felt that." He waved a dismissive hand. "But you don't want to hear about that. Look at this."

He keyed in another command, and she heard the modem click. Seconds later, the screen showed the words *April's Garden* in a vibrant purple font cascading across a pale-yellow screen. A panoramic view of the meadow appeared just below the title.

Her breath caught. It was stunning. "How did you get that picture?"

"I have a digital camera." He gave her a brief smile and scrolled down a couple of inches. A trio of her soaps floated into view, wrapped in lavender print material and mounded in a small raffia basket. Next, a miniature wooden crate appeared, stuffed with her ribbon-tied sachet bags.

He moved the mouse again and the photo of herself in her yellow peasant dress popped up. She read the sidebar.

"Experience the ultimate sensual delight with expertly handcrafted products by master herbalist April Fairchild."

She dragged her gaze from the screen to Tom. "Sounds pretty impressive. I'm not sure I deserve that description."

He frowned. "Sure you do. Remember what I told you about marketing rule number three: If you don't sell yourself, nobody else will, either."

He directed the cursor to a row of buttons at the bottom of the screen. "I've added some Creggan history, a few photos, and most important, your e-mail address and a credit card account." He turned to face her, his eyes bright with the confidence of one accustomed to adding details. "I'll set up the account on your computer tomorrow, and then all you need to do is check every day or so for orders."

"I'm amazed. You did all this yesterday?"

"It didn't take long." He straightened and rolled a sumptuous looking black, high-back chair toward her. "Sit down and have a look while I start the steaks."

She stepped back. "No, I—I have work to do."

His eyes flashed. "For God's sake, April, I don't bite. I'll fix the damn steak, and you can leave right after you eat it. Sit down."

Stunned, she sank onto the black chair and smelled the rich scent of leather. She had to admit there was nothing she wanted to do at home that drew her more than being with Tom. She should get up and leave, she acknowledged. That would be smart, wouldn't it?

Oh, Lord, when had such a simple decision become so difficult?

He started for the kitchen doorway, then spoke over his shoulder. "There's a clean washcloth and towel in the bathroom."

She hesitated. "That's nice. Why are you telling me this?"

"You have a streak of dirt on your cheek." He gave her a long look. "On the other hand, you look kind of cute just the way you are. Countrified."

Tom watched her eyes widen, the blush of crimson color her face. She rubbed one hand across her cheek, then turned back to the computer.

Chuckling, he exited the room. He hadn't meant to call attention to the smudge, but the urge to tease her was hard to resist. He liked to see her smile. He built her Web site because he wanted to please her, plain and simple. It made him feel good.

He mounded mesquite briquettes in the base of the barbecue, added starter, and touched a match to them. When the briquettes glowed white-hot, he slapped two rib eye steaks on the grill. He reentered the kitchen and tore bite-size pieces of lettuce into a wooden salad bowl, sliced tomatoes, then uncorked a bottle of Pinot Noir. This made him feel good, too.

April emerged from the bathroom, her face scrubbed and her hair finger-combed. His pulse raced. Seeing her in his kitchen, scrubbed or unscrubbed, kicked his senses into overdrive. He suddenly realized he liked having her here, to share a meal with him. He wanted her around. Hell, he just plain wanted her.

And he wished he didn't. It was one thing to get turned on by an attractive woman on a casual dinner date; it was another thing entirely to desire one particular female who lived in his backyard, so to speak. For one thing, she was definitely *not* just a casual date. And for another, he'd come to Creggan to be alone and to sort out his life. A distraction like April was just what he didn't need.

He wished he could stop thinking about her. Stop remembering the way she smelled, the things she said. What was it she told him this afternoon that punched him in the gut? If a man was a success but wasn't fulfilled, the victory was hollow?

For the life of him he couldn't remember when he'd ever felt fulfilled.

Until today. Planting roses with April.

He opened a drawer, grabbed a fistful of silverware,

and shoved it into her hand. "Here, you can make your-self useful." Then he raced outside to the barbecue to check on the steaks. He turned them over and breathed in the scent of sizzling meat. He liked barbecuing. He'd also liked working in the garden with April. Odd how such simple things could be so rewarding. Just what the doctor ordered.

Tom shook his head. Dr. Martin had ordered him to take these three months off. He'd come up to Creggan to relax and rethink his priorities, to enjoy himself, and by God, he was doing just that.

Only with April around, it wasn't remotely the way he'd planned.

He brought the grilled steaks in on a platter. Just having April in the same room lifted his mood. He couldn't say why, but sharing dinner with her made him feel good deep down . . . and a little bit afraid. He hated to admit it, but he liked cooking for her. He up-ended the jar of blue cheese dressing onto the salad greens and poured the ruby Pinot Noir into two stemmed glasses.

April looked uneasy. He gestured toward one of the rush-seated kitchen chairs and pushed a glass toward her. "A little Dutch courage?" His voice sounded gravelly. Perhaps she didn't need it, but he certainly did.

He was nervous. He wasn't exactly sure why, but he was. He gulped down a mouthful of wine and forked two slices of meat onto her plate. Alcohol, red meat, and a beautiful dinner partner—all bad for his blood pressure. To hell with Dr. Martin. His cardiologist wouldn't ap-prove, but the man had never seen April.

She settled opposite him and cut into the medium-rare

steak. "What made you decide to come here?" she said suddenly, her pale eyes locking with his.

The question caught him off guard. "You think I don't belong at Creggan?" He eyed her briefly, then spooned a helping of salad onto her plate.

"I did at first, now I'm confused."

"Confused," he echoed. "As in I don't fit up here?"

"It doesn't make sense that a man with your . . . background would want to live in the country. You don't know much about it." April speared a bite of steak and grinned.

Boy could she hit the nail square on the head. He wished he had an answer to her question, but he wasn't sure what the answer was. "Let's say I decided I need to make some changes. Why not Creggan? After all, I own the place."

Her gaze probed deeper. "Do you think you can be happy here after life in the city?"

"Damned if I know. But the city's not *that* far away." *Though it sometimes seems like it's on a different planet.* So far, the only thing that hadn't been a big headache was planting the roses today. He swallowed a mouthful of wine and focused on the shape of her lips. "Besides, I can add whatever conveniences I need."

"You still haven't answered my question. Why did you leave the city in the first place?"

Tom stared at her. What the hell, he might as well get it out in the open. He had to talk about it sometime. "You're right, I haven't answered you. Truth is, I'm trying to figure out some things."

"What things?" She leaned her elbows on the table. "Oh, I take that back. I didn't mean to pry."

He let out a slow breath. "Actually, it might help if

you did pry. I'm having a hard time coming to grips—
What I mean is, I'm facing a situation I've never dealt
with before."

April leaned closer, her silvery eyes darkening, atten-
tive. A ribbon of awareness shot up his spine. Damned
if she didn't look genuinely interested, as if she really
cared about his problems.

Maybe. Maybe not. With April it was hard to tell
sometimes. She wasn't like any of the other women he'd
known. April was . . . unique.

He fortified himself with another swallow of wine.
How much did he want to share with her?

Their gazes met and held. For a long moment, the only
sound was the hum of the refrigerator and the ticking of
the clock on the wall.

Tom knotted his hands. "I . . . quit my job. No, that's
not the whole story." He ran a finger under his collar,
then bolted the last of his wine. "Gosh, I haven't put it
into words before, and it's harder than I thought."

"You don't have to tell me. We can talk about something else, or not talk at all, if you prefer."

He flashed her a brief look. "About eight months ago,
my doctor ran an EKG and didn't like the results. He
suggested I cut down my workload, maybe take a vaca-
tion."

"Did you?"

He sighed. "No. I'd just taken over a new company,
and schedules were busy. Then about six weeks ago I
started having dizzy spells, and my blood pressure went
through the roof. I decided it wasn't worth it, killing myself to compensate for inept management."

"So you're resting up at Creggan while you decide what company to buy next?"

"Not exactly. You know, it's a funny thing about that EKG, it made me realize I might not live forever. I'm . . . I guess I'm trying to decide what to do with the rest of my life. To tell the truth, I haven't a clue."

April smiled. "I could help. After all, if you're getting my business on the right track, the least I can do"—her eyes sparkled—"is keep on asking you questions."

Tom's heart flip-flopped. Having April in his kitchen made him think of domestic things. He liked having her around, liked the way she spoke, liked her ideas. For the first time since he could remember, he'd met a woman who seemed interested in him not for his position or his money but for himself. It warmed him all the way to his toes.

"So what did you think you'd do up here?"

He stared at her. "I honestly don't know. I thought I did, but now. . . ."

"Now?"

"Things I had no time to do before are suddenly very important, but I can't seem to make plans for the future. I don't even know if I *have* a future. Next month I'm supposed to go in for more tests."

"You could be jumping to conclusions. Lots of men overcome stress overload by changing their lifestyles."

"I keep thinking about my grandfather. Granddad died from a heart attack."

"Your grandfather was an old man," April said.

He stared out the window and tried to focus. "Three years ago my father also died from a heart attack. He was only fifty-four."

"Oh, Tom. I'm so sorry. It's a tough thing to face when someone you care about dies. It makes you aware of your own mortality. But I think you've done the right thing. Creggan will be good for you."

"It's already been good for me," he said and grinned.

April's eyes lit up, and without a moment's hesitation, she stood, bent over, and kissed his cheek.

Surprise made him freeze for a split second. An instant later, he stood too and slipped an arm around her waist and pulled her against his chest. "It's been better than good." Then he lowered his mouth to hers.

She didn't resist, but met his lips with a little moan. He deepened the kiss, the blood roaring in his ears. This, he realized, was what he'd wanted all day, to feel her lips against his. But it was happening too fast.

Staring at one another, they drew apart. His heart pounded. In ten seconds flat she had him as hard as a rock.

He closed his eyes and drew in a ragged breath. "I'll walk you home."

"You don't need to. I'm not going to get lost on the way." Her voice shook. Her eyes looked huge, the pupils onyx black.

Heat slammed into his midsection. She felt it, too! The connection between them was like a molten thread. "I want to anyway." He tried for a carefully neutral tone, but he couldn't disguise the raw hunger in his voice. Flipping on the porch light, he cupped her elbow and led her down the steps.

An owl hooted along the path through the redwood trees. Crickets chirped, and through the treetops, the moon shone like a silver globe. Her lavender fragrance made him dizzy with need. His hands ached to touch her.

He held her arm as they walked, liking the feel of her warm skin against his palm. "When I came here, I planned to rest," he told her. "However, I've ended up doing anything but. Funny thing is, I feel great."

Her smile touched something deep within him.

At her porch, she turned to go in but he tightened his hand on her arm. "April. . . ." He leaned closer, pressed his lips to her forehead. Under his fingers he felt her tremble. If she touched him, he would explode.

"I want you," he whispered against her temple. "And I think you want me."

A light flared in her eyes. "Yes, I do. I try to tell myself I don't, but it's a lie."

"Thank God," he murmured. "I want to touch you, make love to you."

She took a deep breath. "I'm not ready to take that step." She splayed both hands against his chest, forcing space between them. She looked at him with clouded eyes. "Not yet."

"What does that mean, 'not yet'? You're ready, I can tell that every time I kiss you."

April slipped out of his grasp. Her silvery eyes looked luminous in the moonlight. "You're making me ask questions about myself, about what I want."

"And that scares you, right? Being with me scares you?" A cord knotted in his chest. Her troubled gaze turned a knife in his heart. He wanted to kiss away her doubt, feel her heart beating beneath her breast, feel her skin on his.

"It goes a lot deeper that just making love, Tom. You know that."

He forced himself to breathe. "Yeah, I know. It does for me, too. I never thought I'd feel—"

"And I never thought I'd want to ever again."

"So, here we are. We've acknowledged we feel something for one another. Where do we go from here?"

FIFTEEN

"I need time," April said. She saw Tom's spine stiffen and read disappointment in the brooding expression. Every cell in her body urged her to touch him. *Why don't you?* a tiny voice urged. *It's what you want.*

For what seemed like minutes, Tom stood without moving. Pain flickered in his eyes. Finally he tilted her chin up and touched her lips with his. Her heart soared.

His free hand splayed across her back, and her body melted into his. "Patience is not one of my virtues," he breathed against her temple. "Your move, April."

"I know," she murmured, her lips pressed against his shoulder. It took every ounce of her willpower not to open her mouth and ask him to stay. She wanted Tom McKittrick. Wanted him badly. And that was exactly why she wouldn't risk making love with him. She felt too vulnerable.

A man's vulnerability made him human, and she liked that in Tom. Her own vulnerability, however, made her cautious. "I'm frightened, Tom."

"I'm frightened too." He drew away a few inches and

stared down at her. "I care what happens to you. And to me."

"I think I could care about you, too. That's why I'm scared."

"Two sleepy, scared people, huh?" He kissed her quickly and stepped off her porch. "Like I said, your move." He strode off across the meadow, and April's heart squeezed.

The roar of a fast-moving vehicle on her drive roused April from her sewing machine. She set aside the sachet bag she was stitching and headed for the door.

Raven's truck skidded to a stop in front of the cottage, and the lanky young man climbed out, clutching a blue-towel-wrapped bundle in his arms.

She propped her hands on her hips. "This isn't the Bonneville Salt Flats, fella. Slow down, there are cats around here."

"I know, babe. Sorry 'bout that." Raven gave her a sheepish grin and shook his ginger-colored ponytail over his shoulders. "I was supposed to be helping Tom half an hour ago, but something came up."

"You overslept again."

"Nah, a more noble reason." He thrust the bundle into her arms. A pair of round feline eyes peered at her over a fold in the bath towel. She peeled the fabric back and uncovered a trembling lump of gray fur.

"Found him in back of Lum's Bakery," Raven explained. "I figure he's been abandoned and you. . . ."

"I already have more cats than I can afford to feed."

Raven tented his fingers under his chin and gave her

an understanding look. "Better here with you than the pound, babe."

April sighed. Sometimes her soft heart worked against her. She needed another cat like she needed a case of poison oak. She inspected its little face, the tiny mouth and nose leather outlined in a darker shade of gray, and smiled in spite of herself. "He is a cute little guy."

"Mrowr." The kitten blinked, gazing at her with saucer-shaped green eyes, and her heart turned over. She ran her hand over the soft fur, stroking it slowly. "There, there." She lifted it out of the towel, and the kitten responded with a loud purr, settling into her arms. She gazed at the animal. "You're the last thing I need, little fellow. But I guess I'll find a spot for you somehow."

She shot Raven an accusing look. "You knew all along that I wouldn't say no."

"Hey, babe. I knew I could count on you." Raven reached out, grabbed her shoulders, and slid his arms around both her and the cat. "I gotta go," he said. He smacked a kiss onto her cheek.

April nodded. Still imprisoned in Raven's arms, she looked over his shoulder into the cold eyes of Tom McKittrick.

"Ol' Tom doesn't like it when I show up late," Raven continued, releasing her. "That guy's a stickler for punctuality."

" 'That guy' has a house to renovate," she said, her gaze on Tom. She watched him step up to Raven.

"I work to a schedule," Tom said. "And you obviously don't."

Raven jumped. "Jesus, you scared me."

"You were . . . occupied."

April detected a tightness in Tom's voice. Holding her arms out, she tried to change the subject. "Raven brought me this little guy."

Tom rolled his eyes. "What a surprise, another cat! Just when I thought you didn't have enough."

April's chest knotted. "I only have nine."

"Ten." He turned to Raven. "You finished here?"

"Did my good deed, so yeah, I guess I am." Raven ambled over to his truck, then pivoted toward April. "Hey, babe, you still coming to the picnic on Saturday?"

April gasped. "Gosh, I'd forgotten all about it."

"The whole gang'll be there." Raven waggled his eyebrows and gave her a mock leer. "If you bring your super carrot cake, I'll be your slave for life."

Tom's face darkened. "Are we going to sand floors or stand here talking picnics?"

Raven tossed him a grin. "Hey, man, lighten up. This is important stuff, too. It's the community picnic—only have it once a year."

He turned to April, his eyes twinkling. "You should ask him along, too. Looks like he could use a diversion." He climbed into the driver's seat, started the engine, and sped down the driveway in reverse. At the fork that angled up to the main house, he jammed it in gear and drove up to the porch.

Tom frowned. "Community picnic, huh? You're going with him?"

April bit down hard on her lower lip to keep from smiling. Tom was jealous! "A bunch of us from the farmers' market do this every year. Why don't you come? It's at the town park. Lots of food, even a volleyball game."

"You're going with Raven?" he repeated.

"I usually go by myself. Unless you want to come along."

"With you, yes. With Raven and you, I don't think so."

"Suit yourself." She grinned. "I thought maybe you didn't like picnic fare."

"Yeah, as a matter of fact, I do."

"Or volleyball."

Tom scowled. "I can hold my own. I'll think about it." He strode off toward his house.

April studied his retreating figure. She'd bet her next meal that Tom McKittrick had never been to a picnic in his entire citified life.

Saturday arrived, clear and hot. April stood in front of the kitchen counter, clad in a pink, cotton sleep shirt as Loreena McKennitt's *Lady of Shalott* floated from her CD player. She loved picnic day with its camaraderie, the good food and games.

The sun's rays poured through the kitchen window, warming her arm as she spread cream cheese frosting on her carrot cake with a long spatula. Milo, the new kitten, coiled his supple body around one of her ankles and peered at Shadow, who pretended to be sleeping.

She extricated her foot so she could reach the nasturtiums she'd washed and set aside for decoration, then pressed brilliant yellow and orange blossoms into the four corners of the cake pan. Beautiful. Raven would love it. And, she thought dreamily, Tom might too.

She padded over to the back porch pantry to tear off

a length of plastic wrap and saw Tom heading her way. He wore khaki shorts and a black, knit polo shirt that molded to his lean torso. She rimmed her lips with her tongue. He looked good enough to eat.

She opened the screen door and leaned out. "What are you doing here?"

He took in her appearance, and for a split second he grinned. Then his smile faded and his eyes held hers in a long, secret look. "I heard the music and figured you were inside."

Her skin began to heat under his scrutiny. Thank goodness the sleep shirt covered her derriere. "I'm getting ready for the picnic."

A light flared in his eyes. He continued staring at her. "I thought, that is, I—" He swallowed and focused on her face. "You sure make it hard on a man. Would you mind putting something on?"

She knew it, he'd decided against the picnic. Then she glanced down at her sleep shirt, backlit by the sun, and gasped. She might as well be parading around naked. "Oh, God. Wait inside here. I'll be right back."

She raced through the kitchen and down the hall, hearing his laughter.

She wiggled into the white shorts she'd laid out on the bed, slipped into a clean bra, then pulled a blue tank top over her head. She felt absurdly disappointed. After all, what did it matter if Tom wasn't coming with her? She'd see all her friends and still have fun. Despite the empty feeling in the pit of her stomach, she rinsed her face, dragged a comb through her hair, and slashed Pink Velvet Mousse on her lips. She gave herself a cursory look in the bathroom mirror, then slid her feet into brown sandals and sped back to the kitchen.

Tom stood beside the counter licking his finger, a sheepish look on his face. "Wow, a five-minute make-over."

She noted a finger-wide groove in the carrot cake frosting, and her mouth curved in spite of her effort to control it. So, the city executive was a little boy at heart. "Very sneaky."

Tom grinned. "You look pretty tasty yourself."

"The cake is for the picnic. Would you mind taking it out to my car?"

"Mine's out in front, all packed. Case of wine, olives, pickles, some cheese. . . ." He lifted the cake pan in one hand, and pushed the door open with the other. "Coming?"

"You're going to the picnic?" Her heart jolted.

"Sure. Where the cake goes, I go."

She grabbed her sun hat and a canvas tote bag, turned off the CD player, and clattered down the steps. Warmth spread through her chest. She had a crazy urge to sing.

He strode ahead of her, the cake pan tucked under his arm, and opened the passenger door of his Mercedes. The silver metallic finish blazed in the sun. He'd washed and waxed it.

She climbed in and settled back in the leather seat while he set the cake in the trunk. The car had that new-car smell, and there wasn't a speck of dust anywhere.

He eased his large frame into the driver's seat, fastened his seatbelt, then checked hers.

He drove fast but skillfully. The heavy car cornered effortlessly, and April found herself enjoying the ride.

She watched him out of the corner of her eye, liked the way his long fingers gripped the steering wheel, liked sitting beside him. Her pulse raced. She wondered how he would fit in with the farmers' market crowd.

"What made you decide to come" she asked as the car sped past the fire station.

"Something you said. About a hollow victory and being happy."

"What's that got to do with a picnic?"

"I'm not sure. But I sure as hell haven't been happy the past few months, so I figure this is as good a time as any to expand my horizons." His expression changed. "Maybe I need a new set of values."

"I think your values are fine. Maybe you just need a new direction."

"Like coming to Creggan?"

"Maybe. Like planting roses."

They entered the parking area and Tom braked in front of a horizontal redwood log. She turned to him. "I should probably warn you. . . ." Her voice trailed off.

"Warn me about what?"

Raven waved to them from a grassy knoll and bounded over.

"Too late," she murmured.

Tom frowned. What should she warn him about? Did she have a thing going with the ponytailed handyman?

He gave Raven a hard look. Purple tie-dye trousers and a black tank top with a skull and crossbones emblazoned across the chest. No doubt about it, Raven dressed like a true eccentric. "Glad she persuaded you to come," Raven said, focusing on April. "Didja bring the cake, babe?"

April swung her legs out of the car and stood up. "It's in the trunk."

"Hey, man," he addressed Tom. "You play volleyball? We're having a little tournament."

Tom hesitated. He'd rather stroll with April. *She* was the reason he'd come. Did he want to play games?

"Some of the players are pretty competitive. Like April, here." The younger man grinned. "I wouldn't want to get her mad at me on the court."

Tom reached inside the trunk for the sack of cheeses and olives, then handed it to Raven. April lifted out the cake, and Tom hoisted up the case of wine. "Where to?"

"First set of tables on the left." Raven set off down the trail, and Tom and April followed.

"What were you going to warn me about?" Tom prodded.

"You'll see soon enough," April murmured.

In a clearing surrounded by redwoods and fir trees, three picnic tables had been shoved together, and a couple dozen people milled about. Tom stopped dead in his tracks.

Two bearded men in leggings and velvet jerkins strolled along the path. One sporting a green hat with a feather waved at April. The woman with them wore a long, red velvet dress with enormous embroidered sleeves and a tall pointed hat with a flowing veil. "Are you sure we're in the right place?" Tom asked hesitantly. "Or in the right century?"

April laughed. "Come meet Lady Alice, Sir Hugh, and Wat."

Reluctantly, he followed her toward the trio.

The man in the green hat extended a beefy hand. "You

must be April's new neighbor. Hugh Wardman. This is my wife, Alice."

The medieval lady nodded. "Lady Alice, when I'm in this garb."

"I'm Mike Watson," the other man said.

Tom shook hands with both men. "Tom McKittrick." He waved a hand toward Wardman. "I feel a bit underdressed."

Wardman gave a hearty laugh. "Our historical music society held a medieval tournament earlier, thought we'd stay for the picnic." He motioned toward the tables. "Set your things down, and have a beer."

Tom settled the case on a picnic bench while April set her cake on the red-and-white-checked tablecloth. Wardman shoved a brown bottle in his hand. "What line of work are you in?"

"Uh, buying and selling. You?"

"Education. I teach chemistry. That is, when I'm not jousting or blowing on a crumhorn."

Raven tapped him on the shoulder. "We're getting ready for the killer volleyball game. Wanna play?"

Tom hesitated. He hadn't played volleyball since his teens.

"Speak up, man. April's team is filled up, but mine is one player short."

Tom had a feeling it was going to be an interesting day. People in medieval robes. A chemistry teacher who played the crumhorn—what the heck was a crumhorn, anyway? And April heading a "killer" volleyball team.

Oh, hell, in for a penny, in for a pound. "Sure, count me in."

SIXTEEN

Tom followed April and Raven, who set out along the path to an open area where a net hung between two iron poles, the boundaries of a volleyball court chalked on the grass.

"Anything I should know beforehand?" Tom asked.

April wrinkled her forehead and studied him. "I don't like to lose."

"Neither do I."

She pulled a pair of grass-stained sneakers out of her tote bag, dropped to the ground, and shoved her feet into them. Then she headed for the far side of the court, caught the ball one of her team members tossed to her, and began assigning positions.

Tom spotted Mike Watson, the man he'd met along with the chemistry teacher. Mike, April's designated server, had shed his medieval costume for black shorts and a T-shirt. Tom studied the opposition—a dark-haired young woman in skimpy yellow shorts and a matching top, three college-age men, and April. Raven's team consisted of six men, including himself.

He glanced again at the players across the net and

grinned. No sense steamrolling her team. He'd hold back; a simple win ought to suffice.

"Ready for the toss?" Raven yelled. He flipped a coin in the air.

"Heads," April shouted.

"Heads it is." Raven pocketed the coin. "Your serve."

Mike Watson drove the ball to deep center. Raven called, bumping it to a blond man named Steve. Steve set, and Tom spiked it hard to the outside.

Watson bumped to the brunette in yellow, who lofted it. April went in for the high hit and dinked it over the net in front of Tom. She flashed him a smile.

Tom blinked. That was a professional play if he ever saw one!

Watson served again. This time Tom was ready. When the brunette set to April, he blocked her spike.

Back and forth they battled. April surprised the hell out of him. She was good. When she spiked, Tom dug the ball, popping it high to Raven. Each time she launched a crippling jump serve, Tom made a dive and sent the ball squarely to the setter, who lofted it to the spiker.

They ended the first game at fifteen to thirteen. Tom grabbed a bottle of mineral water, took a swallow, and dribbled the rest over his face. His shirt clung to his body, a line of moisture extending from chest to waist-line. He hadn't played this hard in ten years. Damned if it didn't feel great.

He watched April help herself to a can of soda. For a woman as female as she was, she was sure athletic. What a fascinating combination of womanly charms and warrior instincts. There were layers to this lady he'd never dreamed of.

She sipped the soda and talked with the brunette as Raven sauntered over and slung an arm around each of them. Raven glanced at Tom and murmured something to April and her teammate. Soft laughter drifted to him.

His jaw tensed. What kind of game was this guy playing? Raven was coming on to April one minute, hugging the brunette the next.

He thought about it all during the next game, which April's team won fifteen to nine. When the final game began, Tom scrapped any thought of playing it easy. If April was going to win, she'd have to beat his team fair and square. No more Mr. Nice Guy. He watched her across the net. Her golden skin glowed in the sunlight, and the shorts revealed long legs with just the right amount of muscle.

He blocked her hit, then came back to stop a short pop and found himself tangled in the net with one foot over the line and both arms resting on her shoulders. "Foul," someone called, and the ball went to Watson.

This time April made the set and the brunette went up for the spike. Raven took the dig, lofting the ball to Tom. He dragged in a quick breath, jumped, and slammed the ball right into the hole between April and the brunette for the winning point. He tossed April a grin, which she did not return.

He had to chuckle. She was a sore loser.

"Hey, man," Raven said. "Where'd you learn to play?"

Tom smiled. "I played a little beach doubles, but it's been a while."

Raven whistled. "You haven't forgotten much."

"A ringer," April said with a mock scowl. "You should have said something."

"What, and spoil the fun?"

Her lips twitched. "I actually felt sorry for you when we started. I didn't know you could play. I even considered. . . ." A moment later she began to laugh, and then they were both laughing.

All at once, Tom felt as if someone had turned on a light inside him. He snaked an arm around April's waist and guided her back to the picnic area where the aroma of barbecuing chicken wafted over them. Tom licked his lips and groaned. "I don't know about the losing team captain, but the opposition could eat a side of beef, hide and all."

Two middle-aged men wearing canvas aprons and wielding giant tongs lifted sauce-drenched chicken pieces off the barbecue and onto stainless steel serving trays. Hugh and Alice Wardman stacked paper plates and utensils on a table groaning with assorted salads, ears of corn, sliced cheeses, pickles, and olives.

Mike Watson hailed Tom. "Have a seat." He indicated a spot beside him. Raven seated himself across from them, absorbed in April's brunette teammate, who sat down beside him.

Tom watched April seat herself, then squeezed in beside her. In the crowded space, his bare thigh brushed hers and her gaze jumped to his, but she didn't pull away. The warmth of her flesh against his made his pulse dance. She had a smudge of dirt on her shirt, likely from their encounter at the net, and another on her nose. The faint sprinkling of freckles across the bridge sent a surge of happiness rippling through him. She was a girl-next-door girl—outdoorsy, natural. Different from any woman he'd ever met.

"April tells me you're doing a little gardening," Watson remarked, spearing a chicken thigh. "She's the best damn flower grower around. Her roses make me wish I'd taken up golf instead."

April turned to Watson, a mound of potato salad on her fork. "Not so, Mike. You're terrible at golf."

A lopsided grin crossed the burly man's face. "Wait until you see my new David Austins. This may be the year you lose your crown."

"You raise flowers?" Tom asked.

Watson chortled. "In my spare time. It's one of those things that gets in your blood, like the historical music thing. I came here to take it easy—a health problem—and look at me now." He gave his chest a resounding thump. "Full-time job, amateur rosarian, play tenor recorder, and organize our medieval tournaments. Been doing it for twelve years."

He popped a morsel of chicken in his mouth. "Not bad for a man who was given six months to live when I got here."

Tom gulped. "That's pretty amazing, all right."

April touched his arm. "Mike's the president of First Federal." She raised her gaze to the man called Steve. "This is Steve Sanders." She gave a low laugh. "You'll see a lot of him. He's my vet."

Steve's smile was warm and open. "How's the newest addition?"

April winced. "He's challenging the pecking order."

"He'll have to learn that Shadow's the boss," Steve said.

Tom blinked. "You remember the names of all those cats?"

Steve chuckled. "Oh, sure. I've seen every one of them at one time or another." He started off, then pivoted. "Bring Milo in for his shots. If you can give him a home, I can vaccinate him."

Steve sauntered off, and Tom looked at April. "That was nice of him."

Raven's eyes twinkled. "Hah. He's just staying on April's good side." He nuzzled his companion. "Kath, I didn't introduce you to Tom. He's the guy I've been working for."

"The help's appreciated," Tom murmured, focusing on Raven's companion. Nice-looking girl in an Earth Mother sort of way.

The brunette set down her chicken leg and offered a hand. "Nice to know you. Next time, I hope you play on our team."

Her forthrightness disarmed him. He squeezed her hand and grinned. "I don't know—"

She arched both eyebrows. "But of course you must. You were great today."

Tom felt his face heat.

Hugh Wardman stepped up and poured two paper cups of wine for Tom and April. "Nice vintage you brought, McKittrick."

Tom nodded to Wardman, then gazed at the woman Raven had introduced as Kath. "This is the first time I've played in years, Miss. . . ."

"Mrs." She flashed even white teeth. "Raven's my old man. I'm glad you came to the valley, Tom. It's a nice community. The people in Lupine Valley look out for one another, like we're all sort of one big family." She flashed April a smile. "Besides, Creggan's kind of isolated—it's good for April to have a neighbor."

Tom let out a slow breath, studying her, then April. "I'm beginning to see that. In fact, I'm beginning to see a lot of things."

April smiled and pressed her knee into his thigh. Tom gulped a mouthful of his wine.

"Yup," Raven said. "One big, happy family. Hugh here lets me teach evening classes at the college so I have my days free to study or"—he grinned—"sand your floors."

"Teach?" Tom queried. "You're not a handyman?"

"Only until I finish my doctorate."

"And you?" Tom addressed Wardman. "You teach at the college, too?"

"Hugh's the department chair," Mike broke in. "And the best damn crumhorn player we've ever had."

"Well," Tom said. "This is a unique community, full of surprises." He glanced at April, sought her hand under the table.

"Don Massey," Raven said, pointing to one of the aproned chefs, "is a retired psychiatrist." He gestured to the other server. "Jess Langhorne is a professional violinist."

"Wait till next year," Wardman said with a grin. "I expect you'll add a bit of interest yourself. Ever run a jousting tournament?"

Raven took the bottle of wine from Wardman and poured cups for himself and his wife. "Go easy on the guy, Hugh. You don't want to frighten him off."

At the end of the day, Raven accompanied Tom to his

car, while April helped Kath with the salads. As they
loaded the case of empty wine bottles into the Mercedes's
trunk, Raven remarked, "I thought you were an uptight
city boy, man. But you're turning out to be regular folks."

Tom laughed. "I guess I am an uptight sort of guy,
but maybe there's hope. I'm finding out there's another
side to life."

"You got that right, man," Raven said, gesturing with
his palms out. "Living in the valley shows you a side
that makes you feel good all over, rather than like something that's been chewed up and spit out."

Raven ambled over to his truck, and Tom watched
April stroll toward the parking area with Kath. From this
distance she looked like a young girl. A very pretty girl.

When she reached the car, he held the door for her.

She smiled at him and slid into the seat.

"You surprise me," she said, as he turned the car onto
the road.

"That makes two of us. I haven't played volleyball
since I was eighteen."

"I didn't think you'd fit in."

"You didn't, huh? Maybe I'm not as stuffy as you
thought."

"Oh," she flashed him a smile. "I still think you're
stuffy. But I also think you're. . . ." She hesitated.

Tom's heart thumped. "What do you think?"

She rimmed her lower lip with her tongue. "I think
you're . . . well, I think. . . ."

His breath stopped. "Yes?"

"Someone who deserves . . . serious consideration."

Tom kept his eyes on the road. His heart pounded.
"Well, that's progress. What's next?"

April laid her hand on his arm. Her eyes glowed with a warmth that did strange things to his insides. "Every time I think I know what's next, things change. You're not the same man every day; you keep surprising me."

"I feel the same way about you. I've never seen a girl spike a volleyball like you do. Scared the hell out of me."

April laughed. "And I thought you didn't frighten easily."

"And I thought you *did*."

Her smile faded. "About some things I do."

"Like?"

She didn't answer. Instead she edged closer to him and laid her head on his shoulder. "I'm still working on that one."

Tom pressed a button, and the sunroof slid back. A warm breeze lifted her hair, and she nestled closer. "That feels nice."

Nice was a totally inadequate word, he thought. A thousand stars twinkled in a black velvet sky; a full moon rose above the line of the redwoods. The night air and April's head on his shoulder kicked his libido into high gear. His blood raced, and he forced himself to take several slow breaths to steady himself.

In the distance, a coyote howled.

April shivered and straightened. "We need to get home. I keep the cats in at night."

"Right." Tom stepped on the gas, and the Mercedes lunged ahead. In minutes, he pulled up in front of the cottage, reached in the backseat for her tote and followed her up the steps. Cats of every description materialized from the shrubbery, pressing against their legs and winding in and around their feet as they walked to the door.

"They wait up for you?"

April laughed. "It's not me they wait up for, it's their dinner."

He stood aside while the cats trotted inside, then followed, setting her tote bag on the table and watched as she poured kibble into three large bowls. The Siamese tried to muscle in and was batted away by the big black tom. "Do each of them have their own special dish?"

"Usually, but sometimes one will—" She focused on the animals, then looked up, her eyes widening. "Pumpkin's missing."

She dashed to the door and ran down the steps. "Come, Pumpkin. Come kitty."

Tom moved to her side. "Can I help?"

She cocked her head to one side. "Did you hear that?"

He listened, but the only sound he heard was the rustle of leaves in the oak trees. "It's the wind."

She turned her face toward the redwood grove at the south end of the meadow. "No, there's something else."

He did hear a sound—faint, like a whimper. "Yeah, I hear it now. Over by the woodpile."

April raced to her car, reached in the glove box and pulled out a flashlight. "Come with me," she said, her voice hushed. She started across the meadow.

Tom loped behind her, picking his way in the dark. A branch slapped him in the face, and he threw up his hands for protection. The beam from her flashlight bobbed ahead, then stopped at the woodpile. Halfway there, he heard her scream.

SEVENTEEN

Tom's heart stopped.

"April?

No answer.

"April, my God, where are you?"

Her sobs carried on the wind, and in a rush of adrenaline he forced his legs into motion. On the far side of the woodpile he spotted the flashlight beam on the ground; beside it, April huddled on her knees. He raced to her, his chest heaving.

On the ground lay the mangled form of the orange-striped cat. April cradled the animal's blood-soaked head against her knees, stroking its fur with her other hand. She looked up at him through pain-filled eyes.

"She's hurt. I'm afraid to move her."

Tom's heart turned over. "I'll get a box and a towel."

He found both on her back porch and ran back, his breath coming in painful gasps.

She folded the towel in the bottom of the box, then lifted the cat in. He hoisted the makeshift bed in his arms and started for the house.

"Coyote?"

She nodded. Aiming the flashlight beam just ahead of Tom's feet, she hovered at his side, keeping one hand on the box. His throat ached watching her.

Inside she headed straight for the telephone.

"Steve, Pumpkin's been mauled by a coyote. . . . Yes, she's still alive, but she's weak. . . . She's covered with blood and breathing funny. Yes . . . there's a gash on her belly. . . . I can't tell. She's not meowing, and she's not moving."

Tom watched the woman across the room from him. Her mouth twisted, and he drew in a ragged breath. Poor girl. Then he glanced at the cat. The animal's life was ebbing. It must be in agony.

"There's no chance?" Her voice grew very quiet, and Tom clenched his hands into fists.

"Yes, I understand, Steve. . . . I know. It's just hard. . . . Yes, yes, I will." She hung up the phone and turned slowly toward him. The color had drained from her face, and her eyes seemed unfocused.

Tom's heart thumped. "April, what is it?"

"Steve says . . . he says there's nothing he can do. He said I should bring her in. . . ." She shuddered.

He could guess the rest of it. Putting the cat to sleep was the humane thing. But his heart went out to April and, oddly enough, the mangled orange animal. "What did Steve say?"

Her eyes filled with tears. "He—he said that her internal organs are probably punctured, and since she is suffering, I should bring her in so he"—she gulped a lungful of air—"so he can put her down."

A lump formed in his throat as he watched her. The agony on her face was unbearable. The vet might be right, but since he hadn't seen the cat, wasn't there a slim chance its wounds were on the surface? That it was traumatized instead of . . . ?

At the same instant, she looked up, naked pain in her eyes. "I—I can't do it. I just can't."

Suddenly she doubled over. Tom reached her in a split second, held her against his chest. He swallowed as her anguish washed through him.

His thoughts tumbled, and in that instant he knew what he had to do. "I won't promise anything," he murmured against her hair, "but I have an idea."

He held her away from him so he could look into her eyes. "If you're willing to let me try something, maybe we can save her."

"But Steve said—"

"Steve didn't examine her."

"I don't understand. What do you know about veterinary medicine?"

"Not a lot," he confessed. He wondered all of a sudden if he was being irrational out of concern for her. "But in high school I worked one summer for a vet in animal rescue. Once I helped with a squirrel who was pretty badly chewed by a dog. It looked like he was a goner, but we pulled him through."

He laid his fingers on her cheek. "It's a long shot, but we won't know if we don't try. Do you want me to try?"

April bit her lip to hold her tears in check. A faint ray of hope shimmered. "Yes. Oh, please try."

Tom squeezed her shoulder. "I'll be back in a minute with some supplies from the house." He leaped down the steps, jogged across the meadow, then disappeared from sight.

April shoved aside a basket of kindling, set the box beside the sofa, and turned on the table lamp. The bulb cast a soft light on the inert form. Clasping her arms around her waist, she paced the kitchen floor, staring at the unmoving form in the box. Her eyes stung with tears, her throat burned. A hollow feeling grew in the pit of her stomach. What if they couldn't save her? What if by trying they just prolonged her suffering?

She stepped into the living room, drew her fingertips lightly across the cat's blood-soaked head. A faint purr sounded in the quiet room. If Tom was right. . . . She squeezed her eyes shut and gripped the coffee table, waiting for him to return.

In the silence of the night, the ticking of the clock seemed deafening. What was taking him so long?

When she could stand it no longer, she slumped onto the floor beside the cat and curled herself around the box. Inexplicably, she found herself thinking about Tom. He wasn't fond of cats. It touched her that he was so concerned.

Just then, Tom clumped up the steps and opened the door, his face a study in determination. Under his arm he carried a canvas first aid kit.

She watched him stroke Pumpkin and speak to her in a low, gentle voice. For a man who didn't like cats, his bedside manner was as professional and compassionate as she'd seen anywhere. Tom had facets she hadn't uncovered. Underneath the city brusqueness breathed a kind, generous human being. And, she acknowledged in a flash of insight, a man who made her feel good, inside and out. Emotionally and . . . well, physically. She prolonged her study of him, aware of a niggle of desire for this compellingly sexy, remarkable man.

He continued stroking and gently running his hands over the fur, checking for injuries. All the while he talked to the cat. "You're going to be all right, little lady. Tom's here, and he'll fix you up good as new. Easy, girl."

Pumpkin responded with a soft meow.

"She's cut up a bit, and her right hind leg seems to hurt her. But I can't find any deep puncture wounds. I don't think she's bleeding anymore." He glanced up. "I want you to hold her while I clean off the blood so I can see better."

April placed the towel he gave her over the cat's body and held her firmly while he smoothed a witch hazel-soaked cloth over the fur. The cat moaned but stayed put.

"You're doing just fine, aren't you, girl?" Tom murmured. "The real test will be to keep you quiet and get you to take some water."

He finished applying the disinfectant and straightened. "She'll need watching. How about I stick around through the night to see how she does?"

He gave April an uncertain smile. "If that's okay with you, I could use a cup of coffee."

April couldn't speak. She nodded, ran cold water in the kettle. She tried to swallow over the lump in her throat. All this time she'd assumed Tom thought she was batty with a houseful of cats.

She moved to where he knelt on the floor and laid a hand on his arm. "Thank you, Tom. I want you to know—" Her throat closed.

"I know. I understand how much the cat means to you.

I figure it's worth a try." His lips curved into a brief smile. "For both of you."

Her heart turned over. "As long as she doesn't suffer. I couldn't bear that." Her eyes burned, and she turned away. "I—I'll get the coffee."

"That'd be nice, but first—" He rose and curled one hand around her forearm and drew her near. Placing his other hand behind her head, he pulled her against his chest. "I know this is hard," he murmured into her hair. "But try to relax, honey. We'll get through this together."

She let his warmth wash over her. He called her honey, a word she'd always disliked, but somehow, coming from him, it felt right. Pressing her face into his chest, she breathed in the musky scent of his shirt. Oh, yes, she needed to be held.

The kettle whistled, and she pulled away from Tom.

"Not yet," he said in a voice she could barely hear. He leaned forward and touched his lips to her forehead.

On shaky legs she made her way into the kitchen to make the coffee. While she waited for it to drip through, she watched Tom carefully lift the box and gently reposition it at the opposite end of the sofa.

She handed him the mug. He lowered himself into a corner of the sofa next to the box, motioning her to sit beside him.

She settled next to him, her thigh brushing his. He gave her a long look, and a flicker of awareness sizzled up her spine. His arm encircled her shoulders. "Keep me company. I need a little TLC, too."

Her heart skipped a beat, and a slow, drowsy warmth crept over her entire body.

He raised his cup. "Aren't you having anything?"

She shook her head. "Can't swallow."

He sipped his coffee and she rested her head in the crook of his arm. "When will we know?" she asked.

"Hard to say. We'll just keep checking."

At midnight Tom awakened April and applied more antiseptic to Pumpkin's wounds. April dipped her forefinger into some water and dribbled it on the cat's mouth. "She's not taking it," she said, her voice trembling.

"She's still in shock. Give her time."

Pumpkin opened one eye, then closed it and lay still, her breathing shallow. April's heart squeezed.

For the next three hours, she dipped her finger into the water glass and smoothed it against the cat's lips. Her shoulders ached, and when she stood up, her legs felt like rubber. She glanced at Tom, flopped on the sofa, his head back, eyes shut. A dark shadow covered his jaw, his hair straggled onto his forehead. Twin lines were etched deeply above his nose.

"You doing OK?" he asked, his eyes still closed.

She stifled a yawn. "OK."

He opened his eyes and grinned. "Liar."

Close to dawn, Tom checked the cat's injuries again. This time Pumpkin's tongue came out and licked the water from April's finger. She looked at Tom. "Did you see that?"

"It's a good sign."

Then all of a sudden, the cat struggled to raise its head and began to lick herself.

He flashed her a grin. "We're out of the woods. She's gonna make it."

April looped her arms around Tom's neck and clung to him. "Thank God." Tears streamed down her cheeks.

"It's okay, honey. You've had a tough night, and you're dead on your feet. I'll go home now, and you get some sleep."

"No. Don't go." She buried her head against his chest. "Oh, Tom, hold me. Just hold me."

He rocked her gently in his arms, then lifted her hands from his shoulders and tilted her chin upward. "You need to rest, and so do I." He started for the door.

"I want you to stay."

He turned to her. "I want to stay, April, but I'm only human. If I stay, I want to be with you."

"That's what I mean." She looked at the tall man before her, feeling her heart open up. Waves of longing washed over her.

Tom took a step toward her. "I can't be around you and not want to be in your bed."

April rose, reached out and touched his arm. "I never say anything I don't mean, Tom. You should know that by now."

EIGHTEEN

"April, if I'm going to stay here with you, it's going to be in your bed," Tom repeated, his green-brown eyes flashing. "Is that what you're asking?"

Her breath stopped. The time for indecision had passed. Slowly, she took a step forward. Then another. He watched her, not moving.

She pulled his shirt free from the waistband of his shorts, ran her fingers along his belly, up the hard planes of his torso.

He groaned. "You're playing with fire."

"I know." Their gazes locked. "Stay with me," she murmured, her voice a husky whisper.

"Jesus. You're sure?"

She smiled lazily. "I'm sure. Unless you want me to change my mind."

For a split second, Tom's eyes widened; then he chuckled. "Not a chance." He drew her into his arms, and she watched, mesmerized, as his mouth lowered.

His lips touched hers gently, then became more demanding, almost fierce in their possession.

"I've wanted you since the day I came to Creggan,

even though I told myself I didn't," he murmured, his breath fanning her cheek.

Fire raced through her veins. She parted her lips, felt his tongue touch hers. Her legs turned to jelly.

"You are one hell of a woman, April." He lifted her in his arms and strode down the hall to her bedroom. Her pulse accelerated, and she began to tremble.

At the threshold he paused, looking from one side of the room to the other. "I've only seen your bedroom briefly, that night I carried you in here." He grinned. "It's just as I imagined it, all feminine and flowery. It tells me a lot about you."

"It does?" she said in a surprised voice. "What does it say?"

He stared at the burgundy-and-lace spread with delicate printed roses, visible from the light in the hall, then the pink and green pillows mounded in the center, the pale rose stippled walls. "It says you're a little bit old-fashioned and a lot modern." He nuzzled her neck, kissed the hollow of her throat. "That you appreciate nice things"—he glanced at her scarred Old English chiffonier—"but value the traditional."

He laid one hand over her breast, and her nipple peaked. "And that you have a very inviting bed." He strode into the room and lowered her onto the spread.

"We could shower off the volleyball dust, or we could just. . . ." His eyes sought hers.

"Let's just. . . ." April rimmed her lips with her tongue, deliberately letting her words trail off.

He pressed his mouth to the hollow in her throat. "You're right. We can shower later . . . in between."

She stared up at him, her thoughts tumbling, her body eager.

He shed his polo shirt, then his shorts, and stood beside the bed wearing only a pair of navy blue briefs. Dark hair dusted his pectorals; a denser thatch spread outward from the center and arrowed down into his underwear. His erection strained against the cotton knit.

Her mouth went suddenly dry. She couldn't believe he was here, in her bedroom, that she wanted to touch him so badly her hands ached.

"Your turn." He bent over her and unlaced her sneakers, then pulled her blue top over her head. Next he unfastened her bra, and her breasts spilled out. She heard his quick intake of breath and felt a shimmer of heat in her belly.

Tom cupped each globe in his hands, lowered his mouth to one, then the other. White-hot flames licked her skin. She raised her hips, and he slid shorts and panties down in one fluid motion.

His eyes turned dark. "Mrs. Fairchild, you take a man's breath away."

She sighed, giddy with pleasure. "I can barely breathe myself, Mr. McKittrick."

He shucked his briefs and joined her on the bed, gathering her in his arms. She waited for his lips to touch her skin, her heart pounding against her ribs.

His kiss seared her mouth, and she forgot to breathe. Desire was like a cord, suddenly unraveling. *It has been so long. So very long.*

He raised his head to look down on her. "I've waited for this. I want it to be right for you, but it's been a long time—" He took a deep breath and gave her a look that melted her insides. "I don't know if I can take it slow and easy."

"I'm scared, Tom. There—there was never anyone before but Teddy, and—"

Tom stopped her words with his mouth. "Forget Teddy. This is Tom. Trust me, April. I know what both of us need, what we both want. I'll make it good."

It was already good. He dropped little kisses on her lips, her chin, then down the side of her neck to her breasts. When he stroked her flesh with his tongue, she gasped.

His tumescence pressed against her hip, and sent waves of heat shimmering under her skin.

"Your breasts are beautiful." He took one nipple in his mouth and suckled it, flicking his tongue over the hardened nub. After a moment, he groaned. "Oh, April, I want to do so much more, but I don't think I can wait."

Pleasure bubbled up from her belly. He wanted her that much! "Then don't. I want you inside me."

Passion made her bold. She had never felt so aware of her needs before, but now, with Tom, she felt gloriously alive, as if her body spun slowly, suspended in a net of golden thread. "Now, Tom. Please."

She reached for him, aware only of her need to be joined with him.

Easing himself over her, he nudged her legs open with his knee and very slowly lowered himself into her. Her indrawn breath made him stop. "Am I hurting you?"

"No." She lifted her hips and took him fully into herself. He felt so good she wanted to cry.

He moved over her, slowly at first, then purposefully increased the rhythm. He drove his tongue into her mouth, moved his hips in deliberate, deepening strokes.

The tiny coil of heat in her belly spun in widening circles until it imploded in a fiery shower. "Tom! *Tom!*"

Spasms washed over her body. She gasped, lifted by a final throbbing surge of ecstasy. White lights flashed behind her lids, and her body felt as if it were filled with an incredible brilliance and floating above the bed.

In the next instant, Tom's body convulsed, and he cried out. His torso went rigid, then little by little his muscles relaxed. He held her tight in his arms for a long moment, then slowly loosened his hands from her shoulders and rolled onto his side. "Thank you," he whispered into her hair.

April curled into his body. "My pleasure," she said, her voice drowsy. "And the pun is intended. I feel like I'm coming to life again after a long, deep sleep."

"You seem pretty lively to me," he murmured, his voice warm and gravelly.

"Lively," she echoed with a soft laugh. "Watch out, I've never felt quite so 'lively.' "

Tom blinked his eyes open to a stream of sunlight and glanced at the sleeping form beside him. Warmth surged through his entire body. He propped his head up on one elbow to study the woman whose smooth, naked backside fit so perfectly into the curve of his body.

Nothing had prepared him for the depth of emotion he felt when he had claimed her. No, not claim, he thought. Wrong word. He'd taken what she freely gave.

The bedspread he'd drawn over them was rumpled, revealing one breast, the mauve-tinted nipple like a delicate blossom against her pale skin. He dragged in a breath of warm, pine-scented morning air. Making love with April was earth-shattering, and it was an experience he already ached to repeat.

But duty first.

Reluctantly, he eased his body off the bed, located his briefs and pulled them on, then padded into the living room to check on the cat. He gazed down at the sleeping ball of orange fur, and a lump formed in his throat. *McKittrick, you've gone off the deep end. You don't even like cats.* Or didn't. Everything seemed different since he'd come to Creggan.

He bent to gently run the backs of his fingers over the soft fur. A purr sounded deep in the cat's chest.

How was it he'd never before noticed how silky and soft a cat's fur was? He rocked back on his heels as a thought struck him. The truth was, he'd spent most of his life deliberately not noticing such things. Like planting flowers with April or a simple picnic among friends.

Good God, what was he thinking? That he wanted April's friends to be his friends? That he wanted to be with April? Wanted her in his life? Wanted her to love him like—

His hand stilled. *Good Lord, I've fallen in love with her!*

In all his adult life he'd never loved a woman. And he knew no woman had truly loved him. When had desire for April become need, and when had this need grown into something more?

He ran shaking fingers through his hair. He had nothing to offer her, not on a long-term basis. His life at this point was in the hands of God and Dr. Martin.

He gave the cat one last glance and made his way back to her bedroom.

April was sitting up watching him, her eyes questioning. "Is everything all right?"

"The cat's sleeping. I'd say she's going to be fine." He sat down on a corner of the bed and took both her hands in his. "But as for everything, I want you to know something. In my whole life, I've never felt so completely bowled over as I do at this moment."

"I'm a bit overwhelmed myself," she murmured. "But I was also worried."

"Worried! Why?"

She gave him a crooked smile and dropped her gaze. Then she leaned closer and suddenly nipped his neck playfully with her teeth. "When it comes to making love, I'm out of practice."

"Ouch! Honey, you don't need any practice." He rubbed his neck. "The hide I can lose. What you've done is take a chunk out of my soul."

She looked up at him through thick, pale-brown lashes and regarded him with thoughtful eyes. "It wasn't intentional."

He studied her for a long moment. "I kind of wish it were."

Something significant was happening to him, some sort of journey of discovery. He didn't know where it would lead, but he knew he wanted to take each step with April.

He swung his feet onto the floor, stood up and pulled her off the bed. "How about a shower now? The two of us together."

NINETEEN

Tom held the soap under the showerhead, then rubbed his hands together to create a rich lather. Happiness bubbled up from every pore of his body. The effect April had on him was the most incredible thing that had ever happened to him. In his entire life he'd never felt so wonderful or allowed himself to be so spontaneous.

He drew his fingers down her neck, over her breasts, smoothing the suds onto her skin. Her indrawn breath made his belly tighten. He worked the lather down her belly to the soft mound at the juncture of her thighs. His heartbeat thundered, and a pulsing ache surged into his groin. *Easy, Tom. Slow down.*

When he smoothed soap over her triangle of curls, she moaned, and in an instant his penis grew rigid.

She took the soap from his hand and began lathering his body, running her fingers slowly over his arms, across his pectorals, along his breastbone. Her touch sent needles of pleasure along his skin. God, if she touched him. . . .

The shower spray gently massaged his shoulders, sending a soapy stream flowing from his chest to his engorged shaft. She lathered his hips, reaching her hands around to cup his buttocks, then knelt and caressed his calves. The water pulsed on her hair, straightening the gentle curls to a waterfall of pale gold.

He watched her body move as she rubbed the soap over his thighs. She had full, high breasts made for a man's pleasure. He closed his eyes and fought to keep his hands at his sides. A moment later she encircled him with one hand, gently drawing her soapy fingers over the rock-hard length of his erection.

He licked his lips. "Lord have mercy," he muttered, his voice gravelly. April laughed, a low, thoroughly seductive sound, and circled the engorged tip with her forefinger.

He stilled her hand. "Better stop right there." He pulled her to her feet, noting the lazy, mischievous look in her eyes, then dropped a kiss on her lips. "I think we need to. . . ."

"I don't." She caught his hand, brought it to her woman's mound. "Touch me."

She waited, watching him with eyes that glowed. Her unashamed pleasure in viewing his body, in her own nakedness, surprised and delighted him. She was honest about herself and her feelings, and he liked that. He liked it so much that he trailed his fingers downward until he found the opening he sought. He dipped his index finger inside her velvety warmth; at the same time he lowered his mouth to hers. She tasted of lavender. "Yes," she whispered against his lips, her eyes closed, her voice muffled by the spray.

Blood roared in his ears. He backed her against the tile wall behind the tub, his erection probing her soft flesh. He wanted her desperately, wanted to take her right here in the shower, but it would be over too soon; he wanted more for her.

It took every ounce of his willpower to pull back.

Her lids fluttered open.

"Not yet, April. There are things I want to do to you, things you want." He tilted her chin up. "There's a better place for what I have in mind."

In her bed he rolled her onto her back, propped himself up on one elbow and leaned over her. "This time I'm going to take it slow. I want to taste every inch of you. If I do something you don't like, tell me."

She moistened her lips. "There's nothing you could do that I wouldn't like."

Heat pulsed in his groin. "Nothing?"

She smiled. "Nothing."

A robin chirped in the oak tree outside the window. The faint hum of buzzing honeybees made him feel peaceful, as if the earth's rotation had stopped just for the two of them. Sunlight dappled the bed. Tom basked in the warmth, closed his eyes for a long, delicious moment. The heat emanating from the woman beside him spread throughout his body, pooling in his groin. Now they would create their own magic.

He brushed a lock of damp hair from her forehead. "Your hair suits you. It reminds me of a golden field of wheat." He drew the top sheet down, folding it at their feet, then sat back to look at her slender waist and rounded hips. The dusky triangle of curls gleamed like beaten gold.

He ran his forefinger down her belly and into the valley between her legs. Gently, he probed her for the sheathed nub hidden in the soft folds. She trembled. "Oh, yes! There," she said, her voice a moan.

Desire burned through his body like molten silver. His groin throbbed; his member grew heavy and hot. She was ready, and so was he. He wanted it to be a thoroughly satisfying experience for her.

He lightly stroked her moist flesh, focused on her pale-blue eyes, glazed with passion. "I'm going to kiss you. Do you want that?" He stroked her again and felt her convulse under his hand.

"Yes," she whispered. "Yes."

Little by little he lowered his head, kissed the inside of each thigh, then drew his tongue languidly along the path his finger had traced. Her womanly scent, faint musk and lavender, made his senses spin. His body ached for possession.

April groaned, and he flicked his tongue in tiny circles over the minuscule button, caressing her tender flesh with his heated mouth.

Her hips contracted. She clasped his head in her hands, pulling him into her. "Tom, Tom," she cried out, writhing beneath him. "I never knew it could be this way. Oh, God, it's . . . exquisite." Wave after wave convulsed her, spasms he could feel against his lips.

The sounds she made during her release sent a jolt into his belly. Had she never had a man do this before? He'd been the first? A ribbon of joy coiled around his heart. Suddenly he wanted to feel her tremble beneath him, to possess her, to hear her cry out and feel her soft warmth enfold him. He'd never felt so driven, so consumed. Nothing before had affected him like this.

He covered her body with his own and drove into her, and his climax swept him into a maelstrom of exquisite pleasure. When it was over and he could breathe steadily, he gathered her in his arms. "April, I wanted to make it last and last for you. Have you never been kissed like that?"

She pulled away, studying him. "Never. Nothing in my whole life ever felt like that." Her mouth lifted into a smile that made his heart sing. "I thought the earth was exploding."

April shrugged into her green chenille robe, tied it around her waist, and floated dreamily toward the kitchen while Tom hunted for his clothes. She cast a backward glance at his bent over form and smiled. By the time he found them, she'd have hot coffee ready, even if it was nearly noon.

She could hear him whistling all the way down the hall. "You Light Up My Life." Humming along, she reached for the canister of coffee just as Raven burst through the back door.

TWENTY

"You okay, babe?" Raven asked, his brow furrowed. "I've been trying to call you for hours, but no answer."

April gulped. "Sure, I'm fine. We—I turned the phone off last night, because of the cat."

Raven gave her a puzzled look. "Yeah, I heard about it from Steve. He's on his way up. I—what's that noise?"

Tom's whistled tune shifted into a scratchy baritone. "It can't be wrong when it feels so ri-ght."

April met Raven's eyes. "It's Tom."

"Oh, yeah?"

"We nursed Pumpkin all night."

"Oh, yeah?" Raven's face broke into a grin. "Hard work, huh?"

April laughed. "If you only knew."

"Hey, babe. Believe me, I know. It's written all over you. You look like you swallowed a gallon of sunshine."

Tom poked his head into the kitchen. "Honey, hope you don't mind if—" He spotted Raven and stopped in his tracks. "What are you doing here?" he said very quietly.

"Hey, man, that's my line." Raven's lips twitched, and

he pointedly glanced at the coffeepot. "If you got an extra cup of that stuff, I could use a jolt. Kath forgot to buy some at Valley Super yesterday."

In tense silence, April poured the steaming brew into two green mugs, handing them to Tom and Raven, then filled another for herself.

Raven took a swallow of his coffee and set the mug on the counter. "Steve told me about the cat. I figured April would be pretty shook up, so I stopped in to check on her—" He leveled an assessing look across the kitchen at Tom. "Didn't expect to find you here."

Wariness tempered Raven's concern, April noted. He'd always been protective of her, even when she didn't need protecting. Tom, on the other hand, looked like he'd been caught with his hand in the cookie jar. She bit down on her tongue to keep from laughing.

A panel truck pulled up alongside the cottage. She glanced out the window to see Steve Sanders making his way to the back door. "April?"

While Tom and Raven stared at each other, she took two steps, opened the door, and let Steve in.

The vet's gaze fell first on Tom, then Raven. "Everything OK here?"

"It's fine, Steve," she assured him.

"I know how attached you are to your cats, and when you didn't show up last night. . . ." His brow furrowed. "I was worried about you after your call. I would've come out but I got tied up in surgery."

"Pumpkin is fine, too." She swallowed a mouthful of coffee, glancing at Tom. He looked like a tiger caught in a cage. She stepped to his side, placed her fingers on his arm. "Tom saved her. He said we could try, and we did. If it hadn't been for him. . . ." She let her voice trail off.

Tom coughed. "I worked for a vet one summer. Learned a few things about injured animals and figured I could help."

Surprise crossed Steve's round face. "I'll have a look as long as I'm here."

"She's next to the sofa, in a box."

Raven set his empty mug on the counter. "I'd better get back to the house. I put a coat of stain on your living room floor this morning, Tom, while you were . . . uh . . . while you were nursing April's cat. It'll be ready for varnish soon." He glanced at Tom. "You want to see it?"

Tom's jaw muscle worked. "Yeah, I'm coming."

Steve ambled into the kitchen. "Good work, McKittrick. Cat's doing just fine. Got some antibiotic salve in the truck you can apply until that belly wound heals."

April gave the vet's hand a squeeze. "Thanks, Steve."

He gave her a long look. "You OK, April?"

"I'm OK. Really."

He stepped to the door, keeping his eyes on her face. "Yeah, maybe you are."

Outside, Tom motioned to Raven and the two of them followed the vet to his truck. He didn't like confrontations, but his relationship with April was his business. And hers. He squared his shoulders.

Steve reached into his truck for a black bag and took out a small plastic tube. "Put this on the wounds twice a day for ten days. That should do it." He glanced at Raven, then focused on Tom. "Just want you to know,

Tom, that we watch out for April. We'd like some assurance that you . . . well, that you mean well."

Raven cut in. "What he means is April's good folks. If she's unhappy, we're unhappy. Today she looks as content as a bear in honey, and we'd like to see her stay that way." He lifted his ponytail out from under the collar of his jean jacket. "Got anything to say?"

"We wouldn't want to see her hurt," Steve added.

Tom let out the breath he'd been holding. "My feelings are entirely sincere. April's a pretty special woman."

Raven chortled. "You just discovering that now?"

Tom laughed, thinking about the night they'd shared. "Not exactly. I learn something new every day."

Raven grinned. "She makes a mean carrot cake."

"That too."

April tapped on Tom's back door. Noise loud enough to drown an explosion echoed from the interior of the house. She knocked again. No answer.

Unlatching the door, she let herself in, balancing a tray of iced tea and sandwiches on one arm. She set it on the breakfast table and went in search of Tom and Raven. She found them in the dining room, Raven sanding the hardwood floor with a power sander and Tom unscrewing the old switch plates.

"I brought some lunch," she shouted.

Tom gave her a thumbs-up, strode over to Raven, and gestured.

Raven shut off the sander. "Lunch at four o'clock? A bit late, isn't it?" His eyes twinkled.

"I missed breakfast," Tom said, heading toward the

kitchen. "Sounds good to me." He pulled out a chair for April, then seated himself beside her. Raven ambled over to a chair opposite.

April nibbled on a bite of her chicken salad sandwich and watched Tom devour his second half. Sitting beside him in his kitchen sent a coil of heat into her belly. The secrets they had shared last night made her long to touch him.

How had she managed to convince herself for six whole years that she wasn't lonely? Being with Tom made her realize how much she'd hidden from herself. She *was* lonely. Cats and roses and friends had filled out her life, and for a long time that had been enough. Now, she was ready for more. She wanted a relationship with a man.

And she'd found the one. Someone full of surprises. She sipped her tea and wondered what she'd learn next about Tom McKittrick.

Tires crunched on the gravel drive as a car engine purred up to the house, and a moment later a knock rattled the front door screen.

"Tommy boy, you there?"

Tom rose to his feet. "Come around to the back, Jim."

Tom led a florid-faced man of stocky build into the kitchen. "April, Raven, this is Jim Rector, my attorney." Tom looked at the man questioningly. "Didn't expect to see you so soon, Jim."

"Didn't expect to be here so soon." He ignored April and gave Raven a brief nod. "Munson wants to meet. Soon."

"Munson?" Tom sent his attorney a blank look.

"Tommy boy, Munson, remember? The Applied Technology guy. You know, the one Carl and I told you about. Listen, he wants to sell." Rector's eyes glinted. "You've got him over a barrel."

Tom turned the glass of tea in a small circle. "I said fifty-one percent."

"Yeah, I know that's what you said." Rector pounded a fist into one fleshy hand. "And you just got it!"

Tom met April's gaze across the table. Her pale-blue eyes clouded, and his stomach tightened. She glanced at Rector, then back at him with oddly detached interest. Folding her hands on the table, she sat back in her chair and watched him.

Jim frowned. "Old Munson was going to take it in the shorts anyway, so he figured our offer was better than walking away with nothing. I told him you'd contact him about your requirements. Tommy boy"—Jim's eyes flashed with sudden fervor—"we have to work out our strategy pretty damn quick."

Rector waved an arm, a gold Rolex gleaming against his pale skin. "It's okay to hibernate in the sticks for a week or two, but you gotta step in now and let those bozos know you mean business."

Tom watched April and Raven exchange a look, and he pressed his lips shut. Why in the name of Christ did this have to come up now? He'd have to fly up there and talk to Munson, closet himself with Jim. Anguish gnawed at his gut. What he really wanted more than anything was to spend another night with April, hold her. Make love to her.

Sure, he liked being successful, liked buying companies and selling off the parts. It had netted him a seven-figure income these past ten years. *It also made you the loneliest man in the world,* a voice whispered.

Once more his eyes met April's. Their gazes held for a long moment, and then she looked away, her mouth composed.

A lead weight dropped into the pit of his stomach.

"I got you an early flight tomorrow morning," his attorney continued. "Play it cool. Don't let Munson know you're really interested. Let him sweat." Rector laughed, a thin sound that suddenly grated on Tom's nerves.

Raven drew his brows together, then scraped his chair back and stood. "That floor's not gonna sand itself." He inclined his head to the attorney. "Rector."

He patted April's shoulder as he passed by her chair. "Take care, babe."

Rector squinted at Raven's departing form. "We gotta sit down right now and work out how we're going to handle this, Tommy boy." He turned to April. "Maybe you could get us some coffee?"

He spun back toward Tom. "I figure we can knock this out in three or four hours."

"I'm not going, Jim."

Rector froze, then broke into laughter. "I must be dreaming," he said between chortles. "For a minute I thought you said you weren't going."

"I'm not."

Rector pulled out a white handkerchief and wiped his forehead. "Don't joke with me, Tommy."

"I'm serious, Jim. I'm staying right here. If Munson wants to negotiate, he can come to Creggan. Tell him anything. Tell him I haven't made up my mind yet whether I want to do the deal or not."

Rector's face turned pasty. "Hey, Tommy boy, you can't be serious. Now that we've found Munson's jugular, it's time to strike the fatal blow."

Raven's sander whined in the background.

"Jim, I need some time on this."

Rector's shoulders slumped. "All right. But I sure as hell don't understand what's come over you, Tommy. Two weeks ago you were hot to take on this guy, and now that we've got him by the balls you're. . . . Oh, I get it." He tilted his head toward April. "She's got her claws into you, is that it? You were gonna evict her, but you got the hots for her instead."

"That's enough, Jim."

Rector's face turned bright red. "Hell, she's only a woman. This deal is worth twenty-nine million dollars!"

"I said that's enough."

"Well I'll be damned." Jim threw up his hands. "Call me when you come to your senses, Tommy boy."

Rector spun on his heel and without a backward glance marched out of the house. Seconds later, his car roared down the driveway.

Tom let out a slow breath and lowered his frame onto the maple chair. Suddenly he felt a hundred years old.

"I gather that Mr. Rector doesn't like the country," April observed, her voice quiet. The look in her eyes made him wince.

"Jim and I have been working to acquire this company for almost two years. When I came to Creggan, we hadn't made any headway." He shifted in the chair and ran unsteady fingers through his hair. Why did she keep looking at him like that?

"Now Munson wants to sell, and I can't renege on my offer."

"Why not?"

He laid his hands on the table. "It's a damned difficult situation, April. I like what I do, and I happen to be good at it."

"Where is this company?"

"Seattle."

Her eyes widened. "So you'd move to Seattle."

His mouth thinned. "I don't know. Possibly."

April set the iced tea glasses on her tray, then looked up. "You know, I wonder what makes you tick. One day you're content to be here and learn about country life, regain your health, and the next you're jumping at the chance to get back into the rat race." She rose and reached for the tray.

"Don't go. We need to talk." He caught her hand in his. "April, this is an opportunity I've wanted all my life. I'm not prepared to throw it away." He touched her chin, forced her to look at him.

"Why is that?" she asked very quietly. She searched his face until he had to turn away.

He got to his feet, paced the room, then stopped five feet from her, legs spread, arms akimbo. "I like it. I like being the best at what I do. It goes back a long way."

April made her way to the screen door, turned, and gave him a long look. "Then you have things to think about, and so do I."

April marched across the meadow, her shoulders held high. Inside, however, she felt as if she'd been dealt a sucker punch to the gut. The more she thought about it the angrier she became.

So much for platitudes about country living. Tom McKittrick was a city boy at heart; he'd never change. She thought she'd learned her lesson with Teddy.

Tom would always be on the go, restless, like Teddy. A man like that had no room in his busy life for a relationship. A woman, yes. A trophy wife. But a partnership? Never. Tom was a workaholic, a takeover executive who lived for the kill. If she fell in love with Tom, he'd break her heart into little pieces.

She stormed up the steps. Thank God she'd discovered it now before she did something stupid like lose her heart to the man.

"I got along fine before you came, Tom McKittrick, and I can again after you. . . ." Her voice trailed off with the bang of the screen door as she headed straight for her workroom.

She plunked a jar of dried lavender and a vial of rose essence onto a plastic pan of basic soap she'd made last week and carried them into the kitchen. Maybe if she buried herself in soap-making, she wouldn't feel so mad.

She sliced the soap into chunks with a butcher knife and began grating each one using a coarse steel grater. By the time she finished, it was seven o'clock and her arm felt like a wooden post. She scooped the bucket of grated soap into an oversize kettle, then added one quart of water. While it heated, she added half a cup of lavender, then poured in the rose essence.

A pungent odor from the bubbling pot suddenly enveloped her. Definitely not rose essence, more like . . . spaghetti sauce. She wrinkled her nose. "Damn." She'd

umped in Milo's garlic tincture and ruined the entire
atch of soap.

She turned off the burner and grasped the kettle han-
les with a pot holder, then lugged the pot outside and
at it near the back step. What on earth was she going
o do with a double batch of garlic-scented soap? "It's
ll your fault, Tom McKittrick," she announced to the
ot of steaming liquid. "I wish I'd never met you. I
wish. . . ."

She sat down abruptly on the step, propped her chin
on her hands, and stared at the redwood tree closest to
her cottage.

She wished she didn't care what Tom did or where he
went.

She squeezed her eyes shut. Tom had shown her the
moon and the stars, and just as she began to believe in
them again, just as she reached out her hand to take hold
of one, he brushed them away for a multimillion dollar
business deal.

She'd get over it. After all, they'd only shared one night
together. But what a night. Even now she ached remembering his kisses, the feel of his flesh caressing hers.

Oh, admit it, April. She'd done the unthinkable: She'd
fallen in love with him.

TWENTY-ONE

Tom shrugged his wristwatch from beneath his shirt sleeve. Six o'clock. His attorney, Jim Rector, and Munson from Allied Technology would be here any minute.

His cufflink caught on the sleeve of his black dinner jacket. He yanked the gold head free and slid the sleeve over his cuff. For some reason, dressing up in formal wear tonight irritated him. Maybe he was more used to his jeans and T-shirts now; anyway, the close-fitting tailored clothes made him feel as if he were in a straitjacket.

He scanned the living room with a critical eye. Getting the place ready for tonight's kickoff meeting had required not only Raven and the painters working full-time, but a last-minute interior decorator to replace his grandfather's worn sofa and upholstered chairs.

He gazed at the new green drapes and frowned. He'd used all his persuasive powers and some hard cash to get them installed on time. Ditto for the beige-and-green Karastan carpet on the newly varnished floor.

Everything was ready. He should feel elated, but he didn't.

In less than an hour, his attorney would bring Stan

Munson up from the airport. Jim had worked out a deal with the Applied Technology president to meet on Tom's turf instead of Tom flying to Seattle to lay out his requirements. Munson had been eager, and now all the pieces were in place. Tom knew he should be enjoying the sweet success of his research, but all he felt was an inexplicable ennui.

He knew the reason. April. From the day he set foot at Creggan, things had felt different. Something had happened to him. Granddad would have said he'd undergone a sea change, but he knew otherwise. April had made him feel alive again.

A white-aproned caterer bustled into the living room, clutching in both her hands a large crystal vase overflowing with ivory-colored roses, pink Oriental lilies, and greenery. The heady fragrance wafted around him. "Where will you want these, Mr. McKittrick?"

He pointed to his grandfather's baby grand piano, angled in one corner, its ebony lacquer polished to a mirror finish. "Over there, I guess."

The owner of the catering service, a plump young woman with burgundy-tinted hair, entered through the dining room door, a notebook in her hand. "Mr. McKittrick, we're ready to serve when your guests arrive. If you'll just have a look at the menu to make sure we haven't forgotten anything."

Tom scanned the list. Smoked salmon canapés, pastry-wrapped truffles, a round of Stilton and imported Camembert, champagne. For dinner, shrimp cocktail, Beef Wellington. . . .

He handed her the list before he finished reading. "That's fine, Colette." Usually he oversaw every detail of such gatherings; tonight he found himself curiously detached. He was far more interested in seeing April.

He glanced out the window facing the cottage, and his chest tightened. He'd invited her. She hadn't wanted to come, but he'd talked her into it. He could understand her reluctance, but for some reason he wanted her to be here with him tonight.

For the past three days, working out the details of tonight's meeting with Munson, he'd struggled to keep his mind off April. She'd been cool toward him, had evaded spending nights with him, said she had work to do—getting batches of sachets ready, preparing a new advertising brochure, caring for her injured cat. It ate at him. All he really wanted to do tonight was talk to her. Hold her.

Now, as he waited for his guests to arrive, he found himself edgy and impatient. It wasn't Jim and his associates and their wives he wanted to see at the moment, even though they were part of his small circle of friends. It was April. The question was, did *she* want to see him? Would she come?

Tom paced the living room floor. Too late to wonder now. Through the window he saw Jim's red Ferrari streak up the drive.

"Nice place you have here," Stan Munson remarked after he, Jim, and the attorney's wife had been shown into the living room. Tom nodded, and over the narrow shoulders of the tall, gray-haired man, acknowledged the high sign from Rector.

Two caterers materialized beside them, offering canapés and champagne. Jim nudged him gently in the ribs. "Thought you had a date for tonight, Tommy boy."

"I do. She'll be here shortly."

Jim scrutinized him with raised brows. "Do I know her?"

"You've met." Tom knew his attorney would not be overjoyed to see April here tonight. Tom, on the other hand, couldn't hide his anxiety. What if she changed her mind?

He tamped down that thought and turned to Munson. "I've worked up a draft for scheduling the transition. We can go over it before dinner if you'd like."

"After dinner sounds good to me," the older man said. He turned a full circle, scanning the room. "You say this place belonged to your grandfather?"

"After he retired, he spent most of his time here."

"Great place to relax," Munson said.

"I'm beginning to realize that. But business doesn't always let us choose where we'd like to be."

"That depends. What did your grandfather do?"

"He owned a brokerage firm in San Francisco."

"And he left you this place?"

"My father died some years ago, and I was an only child." Tom declined the tray of canapés and continued. "Granddad and I used to spend vacations here together before he retired. He got me started in finance."

Munson looked the room over with interest. "With a place as nice as this one, I'd give serious consideration before leaving."

Tom opened his mouth to answer and stopped dead in his tracks.

April glided in the open front door wearing a soft-looking pale-violet dress, low-cut at the neck and nipped in at the waist. The ankle-length skirt was slit to the knee. His gaze traveled down the fitted length of the dress to the matching high-heeled sandals on her feet. Gold clips secured her hair behind her ears, and the waves cascaded down her back in tumbled curls.

His heart leapt. She looked serene and in perfect control. Unlike him, he acknowledged. From the moment she stepped into the room, he wasn't in control at all.

Jim drew near and spoke in an undertone. "You asked your tenant?"

"Her name's April, Jim. Remember that."

Rector raised his eyebrows. "A mite touchy are we, Tommy boy?"

"Excuse me," Tom said to Munson. He strode across the room to April.

April spotted Tom heading her way and her nerves went taut. He looked handsomer than any man had a right to look. She didn't want to see his greenish eyes crinkle at the corners when he looked at her, watch his mouth curve, or see his silver-dusted dark hair catch the light. His black dinner jacket fitted his lean frame perfectly. Her breathing hitched. How comfortable he was in the formal setting.

She looked beyond him and locked gazes with his attorney. Rector stared at her for a moment, then frowned and turned to a taller, middle-aged man who looked familiar.

"April," Tom said, his eyes lighting up. He touched her arm. "I wondered if—"

"I wouldn't come?" His fingers caressed her upper

arm, made her heart pound. She took a steadying breath. "I said I'd be here. I always keep my promises."

"You look beautiful." A hot light burned in his eyes, infusing her with warmth. "Come meet my friends." He wheeled her off toward Rector and the other man.

"April, I'd like you to meet Stan Munson." He gestured toward his attorney. "You've already met Jim."

Rector frowned. "Mrs. Fairchild." He emphasized the Mrs. She nodded and held out her hand to the other man.

"Stan Munson owns Applied Technology in Seattle," Tom explained.

April smiled. "Actually, we met once, long ago. At a reception in Paris. My late husband said Applied Technology made the best engine diagnostic equipment in the world."

"Fairchild." Munson scratched his head, then gave her a welcoming smile. "I remember now. Teddy Fairchild. One of the great race drivers. It's a pleasure to meet you again, Mrs. . . ."

"Just April."

"Well, I must say," the older man murmured, "it's nice to know our reputation for quality is still known in some parts." He launched a sharp look at Rector, then turned back to April. "Think I'd like to sit next to this young woman at dinner," he said to Tom.

April caught the puzzled gaze of Tom's attorney and purposefully focused on Tom.

Tom grinned at Munson. "We can arrange that, but I warn you, she's spoken for." He draped a proprietary arm around her shoulder, his fingers stroking her flesh.

April stepped out of his embrace, her pulse hammering. She wasn't spoken for. For a brief time, Tom had made her dream, but that was all. It was over now. He was leaving Creggan, going to Seattle.

Tom circled her waist and drew her toward a foursome. Before they arrived, he bent down and whispered in her ear. "April, I need to talk to you."

She gave him a brief look. "You do?" She worked to keep her voice steady.

"Not here. I'll figure out something."

He introduced her to Rector's associates, two fresh-faced executives in gray pin-striped suits, striped-navy-and-red ties, and Robert Redford haircuts. Tweedledum and Tweedledee. She stifled a smile. The wives introduced themselves as Lana and Tiffany. Each emptied two glasses of champagne within five minutes, while they chatted about dress designers and Caribbean cruises. April feigned polite interest, then moved on.

An ache welled up from deep in her chest. Tom was too fine a person to waste himself on superficial people. He deserved genuine friends, people like Raven and Steve. She caught him watching her out of the corner of his eye, and she stepped toward him.

"You've done wonders with the house," she said, as he guided her into the dining room. "You've gone to a lot of expense if you plan to move to Seattle."

"April, don't worry about the cottage."

"Actually, I wasn't thinking about the cottage." She seated herself in a velvet-upholstered oak chair at the long rectangular table and gazed up at Tom. "I was thinking about you. About this house and you."

His eyes registered an emotion she couldn't decipher. Surprise? Curiosity? Before he could answer, Stan Munson appeared beside him. Tom inclined his head to the seat beside April, and as the older man settled in the chair, Tom took the seat across from her.

"What do you think of your friend's decision to relocate to Seattle?" Munson asked.

She felt Tom's eyes on her and she turned to Munson. "It's a wonderful opportunity for him." She would not tell him her heart was breaking.

A black-suited young man poured wine while two female caterers set footed compotes of shrimp cocktail in front of the dinner guests. Strains from a Handel suite drifted in from the musicians playing in the living room across the hall.

"I've wanted to retire for some time now," Munson went on, spearing a bite of shrimp. "Just never found anyone I felt could take over the business until now. I was afraid it would fall into incompetent hands, and the reputation I'd built up would be gone. But Tom understands quality. I have confidence in him."

April exchanged glances with Tom. *But you're not just taking over; you're going to dismantle the business and sell it off piece by piece.* Apparently Munson didn't realize Tom's plan.

Tom smiled. "Stan exaggerates. But I think we can work out something that will be equally beneficial."

Jim Rector grinned. "Tommy has it all figured out."

Tom's eyes flashed dangerously.

"In fact I was just saying—" Rector went on.

The server brought in the entrée on a silver platter and set it on a serving stand by Tom.

"Oh, look, Beef Wellington!" Rector's wife squealed. "Just like we had at the Four Seasons last week. I told the maitre d' that no one does Wellington as beautifully as they do." She waved one delicate hand, calling attention to an enormous pear-shaped diamond.

Tom rolled his eyes in a look meant for April. His lips twitched as their gazes locked. She gritted her teeth and concentrated on her mesclun-and-gorgonzola salad.

Somehow, knowing Tom found his attorney's wife a bore comforted her.

Midway through the main course, the chamber ensemble began a sweetly lilting sonata. April toyed with her entrée as conversation hummed around her.

". . . you can't go wrong with Tommy boy. . . . And then the waiter, why, my dear, he just stared. . . ."

She had no desire to join in. She could barely stand listening to the empty talk, could not even look at Tom across from her. She had come tonight because he wanted her to, but she didn't understand why. Dinners like this brought back old memories of the life she'd left behind. More than anything she wanted to escape.

She sneaked a glance at him. With a start she saw he'd barely touched his food. He looked as disenchanted as she felt, and her heart ached for him.

Tom listened without interest as Jim bent Munson's ear extolling the older man's wisdom in meeting Tom's offer. Suddenly, he couldn't stand to listen to one more word. This wasn't what he wanted.

He set his fork down, pushed back his chair, and stood up. He strode around the table to April's chair, then captured her hand in his. "Come with me," he whispered. Her stunned expression sent a thrill into his midsection. She liked spontaneity; tonight she would get some.

TWENTY-TWO

He drew her into the living room and swept her into his arms.

"What are you doing?" April exclaimed.

"Something I've wanted to do all evening," he said, pulling her into closer contact with his body. A current sizzled between them, and he swallowed.

He began a slow dance around the perimeter of the room, to the delight of the three bored-looking musicians. As they passed in front of the double doors leading into the dining room, Stan Munson spied them and applauded; the wives joined in, followed by their husbands.

Jim Rector scowled.

"I have to talk to you." Tom pressed his lips against April's neck and danced her out onto the porch. "I want to be alone with you."

"Alone is nice," she admitted.

"That's what I want to talk about, April. I want you to come with me—to Seattle."

She stiffened. "I can't. I have a business of my own to run. Besides, I'm your caretaker. I can't just leave."

"I can hire another caretaker."

"Why? Why should you hire someone else? You have me."

"You're more than caretaker to me, April. We have something special between us."

She backed out of his arms. "Maybe we do, but . . ." Her voice trailed off. She focused on his dinner jacket, her eyes overbright. "You thrive on success, Tom. Your business will always come first. You love the excitement of conquest too much to settle for anything less."

He closed his eyes for an instant. The truth hit hard. If he didn't love the challenge of the hunt so much, he'd have gotten out of the business years ago. But he did love it. He had his grandfather's blood in his veins.

"April, I don't want to leave you, but this job means a lot to me. I've invested so much—"

She spread her hands in a palms-up gesture. "Then you've made your decision." Her mouth trembled.

"No, I haven't. Not all of it. Just listen to me for a minute." He dragged in a lungful of air. "There's something important between us. Something I don't want to lose."

Her hands drifted slowly to her sides, and she focused on his face. "I know, Tom. I don't want to lose it, either. It hurts to let it slip through your fingers. But you're going to Seattle, and I'm staying here."

He pulled her into his arms once more, moving in a slow two-step down the center of the porch, past the double doors. "Can we change that?"

"Can we? I guess it depends on what we want out of life. Or what we don't want. I don't want another relationship where I can't be myself." She looked into his

ce with troubled eyes. "Seattle is not me. Creggan is
e."

Tom sighed, and slow-stepped her across the floor-
oards. "When I think about who I am, what I want now,
m at a loss. What drove me before was being the best.
Vinning. Now, I'm not so sure."

She stared at him without speaking.

"Now I know that winning isn't enough if you aren't
appy. You showed me that, April. And the thing I'm
eeing in your eyes is not what I expected, and it scares
ne."

"I haven't changed, Tom," she said, her voice matter
of fact. "I've always wanted to live at Creggan and run
ny business to support myself. You're the one who's
changed."

"Don't you see that I can give you financial security?
You wouldn't have to sell herbs at the farmers' market
or wonder how you'll get your car fixed if it breaks
down. Marry me. Marry me and come to Seattle. Let
me take care of you."

"Please, Tom." She turned away. "If I'd been content
just to be taken care of, I could have stayed with Teddy.
It wasn't enough."

The music stopped, and she stood within the circle of
his arms and tried to smile.

"It wouldn't be like that with me."

"I can't do it, live in a doll's house again. Not even
for you. I need to be myself, not play a role. I grow
herbs because that's what I like to do. I like living at
Creggan. I'm in love with you, but I would be unhappy
in a city."

An iron band tightened around his chest. "I'm committed to this project, I can't just—"

"Damn right, Tommy boy," Rector cut in. Stepping onto the porch, he pushed by April and stood face-to-face with Tom. "I'm thinking how stupid we're going to look to Munson if you back out now. Tommy, we've got the bozo in the bag. All you have to do is move in for the kill. Instead, you go all softhearted for some broad who—" He stared hard at April. "Get rid of her."

Tom's hands clenched into fists. "Shut up, Jim. You don't know what you're talking about."

Rector's eyes narrowed. "You're making a big mistake, Tommy. A multimillion dollar mistake." He gave Tom a long, strong look, then turned on his heel and stalked back into the house.

April watched until the attorney disappeared into the dining room. Then she turned to Tom. "He's right about backing out. You might want to talk things through with Stan before your friend Rector changes his mind."

"Munson won't change his mind," Tom growled. "Right now it's more important that I talk to you." He tilted her chin up. "Before we were interrupted, you said you love me. Is that true?"

She bit her lip and studied the floorboards. "I wish it weren't."

"What does that mean?"

"It means I don't want you to go, but I won't try to stop you. You need to do what's best for you."

Tom's chest tightened so he could scarcely breathe. If he went to Seattle, he'd have what he wanted, Allied Technology, but he wouldn't have April. Was it worth it?

If she wasn't a part of his life, he'd be lonelier than ;'d ever been. It would be no life at all without her.

In a split second, the answer was clear. What was ally important was having her in his life, being with :r every day.

He closed his eyes to concentrate, then opened them. April, stay here for a minute. There's something I have ▪ do." He smoothed his fingers down her cheek. "Don't :ave." He pivoted toward the living room and strode into 1e dining room.

Jim Rector halted midsentence and stared at Tom, a vatchful look in his close-set eyes.

Tom stepped over to Munson's chair and spoke in a ow voice. "I'd like a few words with you in the library."

April watched a shooting star streak across the dark-:ned sky, then slide behind the treetops. She clasped her arms around her waist to ease the hollow ache in the pit)f her stomach. Could she bear the emptiness of not be-ng around Tom? A month ago it wouldn't have bothered 1er at all, but in two short weeks her life had turned upside down.

She loved Tom. More than she could imagine loving anyone. Was staying at Creggan worth the heartache of losing him? Could she ever really be happy without him?

The answer was no. Tom wasn't like Teddy, she ac-knowledged. Tom cared about *her*, valued her real self.

And she cared about him.

She made up her mind. She had to talk to him, and she had to do it now. She moved past the musicians and made her way into the dining room. Tom's and Munson chairs were empty.

She approached a caterer. "Have you seen Mr. McK trick?"

"He stepped into the library."

She headed down the hall and tapped on the door. To opened it a crack, then widened it.

"I'm sorry to interrupt, but I have to talk to you. I— maybe we could find a place outside Seattle . . . in the country. Not too far from your office and where . . where I could garden and maybe have a cat?" She fe the sting of tears and brushed the corner of one eye with her fingers. "Now that I've found you, I—I don't war to give you up."

Relief spread across his features. He pulled her inside the room and closed the door. "I just told Stan I couldn go through with it if I couldn't have you with me." H let out a slow breath. "You mean more to me than dozen companies. I just wasn't able to see it until now But, honey, you don't have to move." A light flashed in his eyes. "Stan's given me a top-notch idea."

She jerked her gaze to the center of the room and saw the older man. "Oh!"

"Don't mind me," Munson said. "I'm rather enjoying myself watching the two of you. Makes me feel young again." His seamed face crinkled in a broad smile.

"I don't understand."

"April, listen. Stan suggested something I should have thought about long before now. If I set a capable staff in place, I don't actually have to *be* in Seattle to run the business. I can do it from right here."

"Told him it was just plain stupid to leave something as lovely as this," Munson interjected.

Tom took her hands in his. "I don't know what the future holds for me—or for us. I still have to be retested for the cardiac anomaly Dr. Martin found a month ago. But I do know that it's important that I share whatever I have left of my life with you."

"But how—"

"Stan has an excellent staff already onboard. I've decided not to break up the company, but take over as chairman of the board. I'll telecommute."

April looked stunned. "You're not going to Seattle?"

"We are not."

"You're staying here at Creggan?"

"We are."

April grinned. "I see. You'll implement marketing rule number four."

"Huh?"

"It's more important to be *first* than *best*." She drew him into her arms. "You'll make a one-of-a-kind telecommuting chairman of the board."

Tom's lips curved. "What makes you so sure?"

"Because I know you, Tom McKittrick. You can run a company and plant roses, too."

EPILOGUE

Tom playfully swatted April's bottom. "Time to get up, honey."

She popped one eyelid open and groaned. "It can't be. I just got to sleep."

He grinned and nuzzled the delicate spot at the base of her throat. They'd gone to bed early; sleep had come much later.

"You'll be late for your own wedding."

She sat up straight. "We don't have to be there until three o'clock. Maybe we could . . ." She sent him a lazy smile.

"Could what?" he asked, rolling her onto her back.

Her eyes sparkled, and she ran her hand down the inside of his thigh. "Have some more honeymoon."

Tom sucked in a quick breath. "You vixen." He shifted his weight onto his elbows, dislodged two sleeping cats from his feet, and positioned himself over her. She had made him hard in ten seconds flat.

"I'm never going to get tired of this," he murmured in her ear.

"Oh, I hope not." She wrapped her silken legs around

his hips, and he thrust into her. If he lived to be a hundred, he would thrill to waking up in bed with the sound of robins chirping in the trees and April curled up beside him.

He couldn't believe how close he'd come to throwing it all away. If April hadn't been April, he might be alone in Seattle, staring out on a gray day from a gray condo. Or, he thought with chilling clarity, he might be lying in a velvet-lined casket alongside his father and grandfather. Even now, he couldn't be sure of the future, but whatever time he had, he wanted to spend it with April. In a few hours, with their friends gathered around them, he'd slip a gold wedding band on her finger.

Raven's eyes had misted when he'd asked him to stand up with him. Steve offered to give April away. Raven's wife, Kath, whom April had asked to be her matron of honor, had insisted on designing April's wedding dress. And Hugh Wardman and his ensemble were providing the music for the reception afterward at the park.

April moaned beneath him, and he timed his release to match hers. His body felt completely alive. His muscles bunched as spasms exploded inside him. He cried her name, spilling himself into her in shuddering thrusts. "I love you," he gasped, his voice hoarse. "I love you so much I ache clear down to my toes."

The telephone shattered the quiet. Tom groped for the receiver. "McKittrick," he barked.

"Dr. Martin! . . . Yeah, sure. Test results." Tom's belly knotted. April raised her body up, slipped her fingers through his and squeezed. Worry clouded her blue eyes.

Tom forced calmness into his voice. "What did they show?"

"Your blood pressure is down; cholesterol looks better. I'd say your month of rest has paid off. You're pretty darn healthy."

Tom let out a slow breath. "That means I'm OK?" His heart started beating again. April's eyes filled, and she bit her lip.

"But a little advice," the doctor went on. "I want you to relax—"

"Oh, right. Relax. Um, I've just been doing that." He looked at April and smiled.

"And get regular exercise."

"Sure thing, Doc. We've—I've been exercising." He grinned at April.

"Above all, make sure you do things that are fun."

"Fun, you say?" He curled one hand around April's shoulder and pulled her against his chest. "Oh, you bet. Don't worry on that count." He hung up the phone.

"No more honeymoon?" she said with a slow smile.

Tom tilted her chin up and kissed her lips. "Dr. Martin's prescription is relaxation, regular exercise, and doing things that are fun. Now, I think," he said with a smile, glancing at the bedside clock and dragging her down onto the sheet, "that we have just enough time for all three."

"And tomorrow," April said, her eyes twinkling, "we'll do things more in line with what Dr. Martin really had in mind."

Tom paused and searched her face. "What things?"

"You'll work at your computer, I'll transplant my basil seedlings, and we'll both pick roses for the county fair."

ABOUT THE AUTHOR

Suzanne Barrett lives in the mountains eight miles above the coastal town of Santa Cruz, California, with her husband, a dog, and three cats. Formerly a facility engineer, she left the stress of a high-tech job to write full-time. In addition, she enjoys gardening and cooking, and creating content for her own Irish travel Web site for About.com.

Hearts At Risk is her third book for Kensington's Zebra Bouquet line, and once again she returns to the Northern California setting with which she is so familiar.

Suzanne loves to create short stories of warmth and passion, and she loves to travel. Heaven for her is a West Cork cottage overlooking the Irish Sea.

She is a member of the Romance Writers of America and is the recipient of the Region 6 Service Award. She was a three-time Golden Heart finalist and has won numerous writing contests.

Write to Suzanne at P.O. Box 324, Felton, CA 95018 or e-mail her at sbarrett@cruzio.com

With an SASE, readers may request a copy of her newsletter, "Romance and Roses."

BOOK YOUR PLACE ON OUR WEBSITE AND MAKE THE READING CONNECTION!

We've created a customized website just for our very special readers, where you can get the inside scoop on everything that's going on with Zebra, Pinnacle and Kensington books.

When you come online, you'll have the exciting opportunity to:

- View covers of upcoming books
- Read sample chapters
- Learn about our future publishing schedule (listed by publication month *and author*)
- Find out when your favorite authors will be visiting a city near you
- Search for and order backlist books from our online catalog
- Check out author bios and background information
- Send e-mail to your favorite authors
- Meet the Kensington staff online
- Join us in weekly chats with authors, readers and other guests
- Get writing guidelines
- AND MUCH MORE!

Visit our website at
http://www.zebrabooks.com

More Zebra Regency Romances

__A Noble Pursuit by Sara Blayne   **$4.99**US/**$6.50**CAN
   0-8217-5756-3

__Crossed Quills by Carola Dunn   **$4.99**US/**$6.50**CAN
   0-8217-6007-6

__A Poet's Kiss by Valerie King   **$4.99**US/**$6.50**CAN
   0-8217-5789-X

__Exquisite by Joan Overfield   **$5.99**US/**$7.50**CAN
   0-8217-5894-2

__The Reluctant Lord by Teresa Desjardien   **$4.99**US/**$6.50**CAN
   0-8217-5646-X

__A Dangerous Affair by Mona Gedney   **$4.50**US/**$5.50**CAN
   0-8217-5294-4

__Love's Masquerade by Violet Hamilton   **$4.99**US/**$6.50**CAN
   0-8217-5409-2

__Rake's Gambit by Meg-Lynn Roberts   **$4.99**US/**$6.50**CAN
   0-8217-5687-7

__Cupid's Challenge by Jeanne Savery   **$4.50**US/**$5.50**CAN
   0-8217-5240-5

__A Deceptive Bequest by Olivia Sumner   **$4.50**US/**$5.50**CAN
   0-8217-5380-0

__A Taste for Love by Donna Bell   **$4.99**US/**$6.50**CAN
   0-8217-6104-8

Call toll free **1-888-345-BOOK** to order by phone or use this coupon to order by mail.

Name_____

Address_____

City _____ State _____Zip_____

Please send me the books I have checked above.

I am enclosing	$_____
Plus postage and handling*	$_____
Sales tax (in New York and Tennessee only)	$_____
Total amount enclosed	$_____

*Add $2.50 for the first book and $.50 for each additional book.

Send check or money order (no cash or CODs) to:

Kensington Publishing Corp., 850 Third Avenue, New York, NY 10022

Prices and Numbers subject to change without notice.

All orders subject to availability.

Check out our website at **www.kensingtonbooks.com**